"I fly to Kona at noon."

They weren't alone in the long, elegant hallway, but, for Ashley, it seemed they were the only two people on earth. Tonio studied her for a long moment, his gaze unnerving. She felt awkward, unstrung, like a girl on her first date, reluctant to let her beloved go.

"May I give you a good-bye hug now?" he asked as he drew her into his arms. "Things will be crowded and hectic tomorrow."

Before she could utter a sound, he wrapped his arms around her. She loved the delicious warmth of his embrace.

"This isn't good-bye, Ashley," he whispered. "I'm counting on us being together again." He lowered his face to hers and brushed a kiss against her cheek.

Surprised, she turned her head, only to find his lips touching hers.

CAROLE GIFT PAGE resides in Southern California with Bill, her husband of forty-two years. This award-winning author of forty-five books once had a job sculpting heads out of clay for a man who made ventriloquist dummies. Today, Carole teaches and speaks at churches and conferences across the country on the topic of "Becoming a Woman of Passion." She and her sister Susan, a talented singer and ventriloquist, have formed a "Sister Act" and perform often for women's programs and retreats. Susan is accompanied by "Sam," whose head Carole sculpted. Carole also draws from her book *Misty*, about the death of her fourth child—a newborn baby, to share how God can bring us amazing joy in the midst of our deepest sorrows.

Carole taught creative writing at Biola University, La Mirada, California, and is on the Advisory Board of the American Christian Writers. She received the C. S. Lewis Honor Book Award and was a finalist several times for the prestigious Gold Medallion and Campus Life Book-of-the-Year Award. Besides Misty, Carole and Bill have three other children—Kimberle, David, and Heather—and four darling grandchildren.

Books by Carole Gift Page

HEARTSONG PRESENTS
HP570—Beguiling Masquerade

Don't miss out on any of our super romances. Write to us at the following address for information on our newest releases and club information.

Heartsong Presents Readers' Service
PO Box 721
Uhrichsville, OH 44683

Or visit www.heartsongpresents.com

By the
Beckoning Sea

Carole Gift Page

Heartsong Presents

To my beautiful daughter, Heather Gift Lillengreen, who as a newlywed living in Hawaii shared with me her knowledge and love of the Big Island. And thanks to Heather and Adam for giving the "grand tour" of that tropical paradise.

A note from the Author:
I love to hear from my readers! If you would like a reply, please include your e-mail address. You may correspond with me by writing:

Carole Gift Page
Author Relations
PO Box 721
Uhrichsville, OH 44683

ISBN 978-1-60260-076-8

BY THE BECKONING SEA

All scripture quotations are taken from the HOLY BIBLE, NEW INTERNATIONAL VERSION®. NIV®. Copyright © 1973, 1978, 1984 by International Bible Society. Used by permission of Zondervan Publishing House. All rights reserved.

All of the characters and events in this book are fictitious. Any resemblance to actual persons, living or dead, or to actual events is purely coincidental.

Our mission is to publish and distribute inspirational products offering exceptional value and biblical encouragement to the masses.

PRINTED IN THE U.S.A.

prologue

Mr. & Mrs. Alexander Bancroft
cordially invite you to share their joy
at the marriage of their daughter
Miss Ashley Bancroft
to Mr. Bennett Radison
at 5:00 p.m.
on the third Saturday of June
at the Hilton Hawaiian Village on Waikiki Beach
Honolulu, Hawaii
Beach reception and luau following ceremony

one

Ashley Bancroft would remember her wedding day for the rest of her life—the cluster of family and friends gathered on the white sandy beach near the jutting lava rock wall; the panoramic view of the deep blue Pacific Ocean at dusk; and the distant, majestic Diamond Head volcano framed by Hawaii's lush green, palm-fringed coastline.

The fragrance of blooming bougainvillea and plumeria trees mingled in the evening breeze with the pungent scents of orchids and lilies in Ashley's bridal bouquet. She could hear the ukulele player strumming the "Hawaiian Wedding Song." She could smell the smoked kalua pig and sweet potatoes roasting in the luau pit nearby.

And she could see her beloved Ben facing her in his black cutaway tuxedo with the customary green leafy lei draped around his neck. Those moments were like a dream now, full of possibility and romance—she in her strapless satin A-line gown with its beaded embroidery and lace, her hair wreathed in hibiscus, her rhinestone sandals sinking into the soft white sand as Pastor Kealoha led them in their vows. The images were etched indelibly on her mind's eye—vivid, surreal, and now utterly painful.

Diamond Head was the only thing that didn't erupt the day that her cherished dreams shattered into a nightmare.

And yet it had all started out so beautifully.

She could still hear Pastor Kealoha's voice rising and falling with a predictable, lyrical drone. He obviously loved weddings, for he was waxing eloquent, as if performing for some unseen theater critic. She could imagine some reality show judge pronouncing him a natural thespian, or an impossible ham, or just plain boring.

For some reason she couldn't focus on his words, couldn't make sense of them, although she knew they were important, something about God's plan and purpose for the home. She needed to comprehend their meaning—this was crucial—make the words her own, make them real to her, but they seemed just beyond her grasp.

It was all she could do to keep her ankles from wobbling, to keep her sandaled feet from sinking into the shifting sand. *Relax*, she told herself. *This is the best day of your life. Enjoy it.*

She wanted to enjoy it but felt too light-headed, her stomach unsettled. At dusk, the tropical air was heavy and warm, stealing her breath. She couldn't see her family and friends now—they were behind her—but she could feel their presence, sense them surrounding her, pressing in on her with all their hopes and expectations. Or maybe the problem was her lace bodice; the gown was cinched too tightly at the waist. Was it possible she had gained weight since her fitting?

She wondered, *What if I faint dead away at Ben's feet?* She had seen television videos of wedding disasters—grooms fainting, brides falling into their wedding cakes.

She stole a glance at Ben. He looked as discomfited as she. He was a lean, graceful man with short-cropped, straw-blond hair, a ruddy complexion, and a ready smile. Wire-rimmed spectacles framed merry, half-moon hazel eyes. But now perspiration beaded his high forehead and upper lip. His jaw was set, jutting forward, as if he were grinding his teeth.

It's not supposed to be this way. Everything should be perfect.

She closed her eyes. Her moist palms tightened around her bridal bouquet. *Lord, this is what You want for me, isn't it?*

Pastor Kealoha's voice caught her off guard. He was instructing the happy couple to face each other and recite their vows. She handed her bouquet to her maid of honor, her best friend, Dixie Salinger, then turned and faced Ben as he took her hands in his. With only a slight tremor in her voice, she repeated the words she had carefully written and memorized.

"Ben, when I first moved to New York City three years ago and started working for Haricott Publishing, I was just a timid, small-town girl striking out on her own. I never imagined I'd meet the man of my dreams. When you hired me as your editorial assistant, I was thrilled to be working for such a distinguished and renowned editor. Bennett Radison, the talk of the literary world. Every woman in the office was jealous of me working so closely with you. At first, I was in awe of you, afraid of doing something to displease you. But then, as we became friends, I realized what a remarkable man you are—considerate, creative, strong, stubborn, smart."

She drew in a quick breath, her heart pounding so hard she could hardly hear her own voice. "We—we have so much in common, Ben. We both love good literature. We love taking a walk in the park after a long day's work and splitting a mushroom pizza while we watch the late show. I don't even mind when you critique my feeble attempts at writing the Great American Novel. You are the man I want to be my husband and the father of my children someday—a loyal, loving, godly man who will be by my side for the rest of my life."

Her words hung in the air for a long minute. It was Ben's turn now. Pastor Kealoha nodded. The silence lengthened, becoming uncomfortable. Ben tightened his grip on her hands as her eyes searched his. There was something in his eyes she couldn't read, a dark intensity, as if he were struggling with something deep in his soul.

"Ben," she whispered, "if you've forgotten your vows, just say what's on your heart."

He nodded and cleared his throat, then spoke over rising emotion. "Ash—my beautiful Ashley. I love so much about you—your kindness, your wit, your passion for life, your devotion to your work, your deep faith, your generous spirit. I love the way the sun turns your hair golden and the moon puts little blue stars in your eyes.

"I remember the first time I saw you, I couldn't take my eyes off you. You weren't like other women in the office in their drab business suits and no-nonsense hairdos. You looked like a free spirit in your bright, trendy clothes and long, crimped curls. I pictured you running through a meadow with the wind in your hair. As if you weren't quite real. As if I'd imagined you—an illusion, a fantasy. I thought you were a lightweight. I didn't expect you to last long. But you blew me away with your first editing assignment. You were good. Amazing. You still are. I can always count on you to do your best, to be true to yourself, true to God, and true to everyone around you.

"I can't tell you how happy I've been to have you in my life. You've changed me, made me a better man. You've made me realize things about myself I never knew. You've taught me the importance of utter, absolute honesty, even when it hurts. That's why. . ."

He stopped, his expression darkening. His eyes broke away from hers. But not before she glimpsed something in them that knotted her stomach and sent her heart racing with panic and dread. She felt her smile freeze on her lips. Everything was slipping away, her future collapsing around her, the whole world suddenly off-kilter. Nothing had happened; yet everything was different. She knew it was over before Ben even said the words.

"I'm sorry. I can't do this, Ash."

"Don't," she implored.

"I love you. I'll always love you. But I'm not the man for you." He circled her waist with his arm and turned her toward their wedding guests, as if this were a natural part of the ceremony. She could hardly make out the sea of faces through her tears.

"It's my fault," Ben told everyone in his most sonorous voice. "I'm sorry. There won't be a wedding today. But please stay for the luau. The tables are brimming with island delicacies— lobster and mahimahi, pineapples, poi, seviche. Enjoy the food and fellowship." Had he actually said *fellowship*? That was her word, not his. He gazed down, his eyes entreating her. "Please don't hate me."

Before she could find her voice, he began walking her down the flower-strewn pathway just the way they were supposed to do, except without music, without a marriage, with only the stunned silence of their family and friends heavy in the air.

The rest of the evening was a blur—a cacophony of sounds, a crazy quilt of colors, a kaleidoscope of motion as the wedding guests milled around on the beach, sampled the sweet guava juice and virgin mai tais, then gathered around the roasting pit for the luau.

But Ashley wanted no part of the festivities.

"Let me go back to the hotel," she begged Ben.

"Not until we've talked. Let's take a walk down the beach. Somewhere private."

She removed her sandals and tossed them aside, then gathered her satin gown up around her knees. He pulled off his shoes and socks, rolled up his pant legs, then took her arm firmly in his. Surely they made a peculiar sight as they strolled barefoot along the water's edge. When they found an isolated cove, they sat down on a smooth outcropping of rock, where the waves washed in over their feet. She thought fleetingly of protecting her wedding dress, then dismissed the idea. It wasn't as if she needed it anymore. They sat side by side, close enough that their arms touched, yet worlds apart. The muggy night air was electric with unspoken words, unshed tears.

Minutes ago they were ready to pledge their undying love. Now they were like colliding strangers trying to extricate themselves from one another.

She forced out the words, "You don't want to marry me. What else is there to say?"

"Plenty."

She didn't want to hear it. For the first time she wished Ben was like other men who grunted single-syllable replies. But not her Ben. He loved words. He analyzed everything to death. Even their marriage. Or *near* marriage.

"We've had a good thing going, Ash." He massaged his knuckles, weighing his words. "I loved the idea that you were a pure Christian girl with high standards and values. From the beginning I've tried to measure up to what you expected of me."

"And you have, Ben. You've always been a perfect gentleman. We share the same values, the same faith. That's what I love about you."

"That's just it, Ash." He reached over and squeezed her hand hard. The sky was darkening, with strokes of violet and crimson slashing the horizon. Ben's voice broke, husky, uneven. "I've tried to be the person you wanted. I did the whole church bit. I thought I could make it work. But it's not me. I'm not into this whole Jesus thing like you are. The truth is, I don't get it. And today when I stood at the altar looking at you, I knew I couldn't sentence you to a life with a man pretending to be something he wasn't. You deserve the truth. You deserve a man who lives his faith the way you do. But I'm not that man."

Whatever else Ben said fell on deaf ears. Ashley wasn't there, was no longer conscious of her surroundings, or of Ben's presence, or of the sounds and voices drifting from the luau. She could think only that she was the victim of a terrible joke. Surely everyone was laughing, and nothing in her life would ever be right again.

two

Bennett Radison flew home to New York early the next morning. Ashley spent her so-called wedding night alone in the bridal suite of her beachfront hotel. Not alone actually. Her parents stayed with her, alternately offering comfort and warm milk—her mother's solution to every distress—and decrying Bennett Radison for his cruelty and callousness. "You're better off without that heel," her mother said over and over as she fluffed Ashley's pillow or stroked her forehead.

Ashley didn't want to hear it. She wanted sleep—a deep, soothing slumber that would erase all the pain and memories of the past few hours. But sleep eluded her, taunted her with brief moments of dreamy repose—only to startle her awake with shards of bitter reality. *Ben doesn't want me. He's forsaken me. How could God let this happen?*

Her mother didn't help matters, the way she hovered over Ashley like an anxious nursemaid, reassuring her, "God will bring a wonderful man into your life, sweetheart. Just you wait and see."

Pulling the pillow over her head to block out her mother's voice, Ashley shrilled, "I don't want another man! I want Ben!"

But Ben was gone.

The next day Ashley convinced her parents to go home without her. "Don't worry, I won't be alone. Dixie promised to stay in Hawaii with me for a few days. We'll do some sightseeing and catch up on old times," she said with more bravado than she felt.

"Well, if anyone can cheer you up, it's Dixie. She's such a funny, eccentric girl. But after that, what will you do, honey?" Her mother's face looked pinched with worry and lined with wrinkles Ashley hadn't noticed before.

"I don't know, Mom. I can't go back to New York yet. How can I face people? I don't have a husband. I won't even have a job."

"Of course you have a job. Everyone at Haricott Publishing loves you."

"Not Ben. There's no way I'm going back to work as Ben's editorial assistant. I'll have to find another job."

Ashley told her friend Dixie the same thing that afternoon as the two sat in lounge chairs on the hotel lanai, sipping sodas and gazing out at the vast, cerulean-blue ocean. "I'm not going back to New York, Dix. I'm moving somewhere else."

"Where?" Dixie's dark brown eyes flashed with astonishment. "You love New York. Your whole life is there."

"Not anymore. Ben was my world. Without him, everything else is meaningless."

Frown lines furrowed Dixie's pixie face. She set down her glass, her apple-red lips pursing in an exaggerated pout. "That's not my best bud talking. Who are you? What did you do with Ashley Bancroft, the gal who faces every trial with such amazing faith?"

Ashley flattened her straw between her teeth. She wasn't sure she could cope with Dixie today—bouncy, bubbly, exhausting Dixie. As much as Ashley adored her ditzy, freewheeling, heart-of-gold pal, sometimes Dixie was a downright pain. "You're questioning my faith just because I don't want to go back and work for the man who rejected me in front of the whole world?"

"Not quite the whole world, Ash. Just family and friends and a few hotel employees."

"You know what I mean."

"Oh, and Pastor Kealoha, of course, but he's cool. He wouldn't—"

"Stop it, Dix. I've made up my mind. I'm going somewhere where no one looks at me with pity."

Dixie reached over and squeezed Ashley's hand. "Just one request, girlfriend. Don't make any permanent decisions for a few months. Give yourself time to heal."

"You make it sound like I've got a disease."

"The scourge of the broken heart. But they say it's not fatal."

"Says who?"

"Wiser folks than me. Doesn't the Bible say something about God healing the brokenhearted?"

"I know all the verses. Jesus bore our sorrows. He loves me and will never leave me." Tears gathered behind Ashley's eyes, pressing so hard her head ached. She spoke over a rising sob. "Then why does it hurt so much, Dixie? Why do I feel so abandoned?"

"I don't know. But I'm not going anywhere, Ash. Just tell me how I can help."

Ashley pulled a tissue from the pocket of her terrycloth robe. The robe was provided by the hotel, so at least she didn't have to wear her satin honeymoon lingerie. She blew her nose and swiped at her tears. "When I was a kid in Sunday school, it was so easy to sing all the songs. 'Jesus is all I need.' 'I surrender all.' 'You can have the whole world, but give me Jesus.' But how do I live those words, Dixie? The truth is, I don't know how to give up everything for Jesus. I don't even know how to give up Ben!"

"We'll start by doing stuff to take your mind off that big lug."

"What stuff?"

Dixie shrugged. "We're here in Hawaii. We'll go sightseeing. How long can you keep this hotel room?"

"Two weeks. It's already paid for. Ben told me to stay and enjoy it—as if I could."

"Why not? We could have a lot of fun in two weeks."

Ashley sighed. "And then there's the cruise."

"Cruise?"

"Ben signed us up for a ten-day cruise around the islands.

It's not for two weeks yet, so we were going to do the tourist bit first, then take the cruise."

"I'm surprised your workaholic Ben was willing to take that much time away from the office."

"He had his bases covered with the rest of the staff. Besides, he had ulterior motives. Anthony Adler, one of Haricott's best-selling authors, is doing a lecture series on the ship. Ben figured we could combine business and pleasure. Go on our honeymoon and talk with Adler about his upcoming book."

"Anthony Adler? I've heard of him."

"He's been on the *New York Times* best-seller list. I love his novels, especially the ones set in Hawaii. He tells such a great story. So full of action and emotion. And they're never smutty. He manages to make 'wholesome' exciting."

"Hey, you're really impressed with this guy."

"I did some line editing on his latest books, and I've talked with him on the phone a few times. He's quite an extraordinary man."

"Come to think of it, I've seen his picture on his books. He's not bad on the eyes."

"He has a beautiful soul. When you read him, you feel like he really understands a woman's heart." Ashley gazed off into the distance, her voice softening. "I was really looking forward to meeting him and getting a few pointers about my own writing. Ben's helped me with my novel, of course, but I'd love a seasoned author's opinion. Now that'll never happen."

"Why not?"

"Because I'll have to cancel the cruise."

"No, you don't."

"Yes, I do. I can't go without Ben."

"Didn't he tell you to enjoy your honeymoon because everything's already paid for?"

"Yes, but. . ."

"Then let's go."

"Who? The two of us?"

"Sure. I've got the time. That's one advantage of having my own cosmetics business. I can ask myself, 'Dixie Salinger, may I take off work to go on a cruise?' And my alter ego replies, 'Absolutely, Dixie Salinger. Go and have a wonderful time.'"

Ashley shook her head. "It's a crazy idea. Totally insane."

"You want to meet Anthony Adler, don't you?"

"Yes." She felt herself weakening. Why did she always give in to Dixie's screwball schemes?

"Then call the cruise line and change one ticket from Ben's name to mine."

A sprig of hope blossomed in Ashley's heart. "We *could* do it, couldn't we?"

"We *will* do it! Or my name's not Dixie Salinger."

Ashley laughed, surprising herself. "There must be a fate worse than taking your honeymoon cruise with your best friend instead of the man of your dreams, but I don't know what it is!"

ॐ

And that's how Ashley Bancroft found herself at the Honolulu harbor two weeks later, boarding the magnificent *Sea Queen*, with fun-loving, free-spirited Dixie Salinger. They stifled chuckles of amazement as the attendant showed them to their luxurious suite with its king-size beds, sprawling balcony, and panoramic windows.

If Ashley had qualms about taking the cruise with Dixie, her anxieties dissipated as the excitement and welcoming ambience of the ship enveloped them. They followed the crowd to the pool deck and had a delicious buffet lunch at the Oceanview Café, then went back to their stateroom and unpacked. When the alarm sounded just before sailing, they pulled on their bulky life jackets and joined the other passengers for the emergency lifeboat drill. They sipped frosty tropical fruit drinks at the sail-away party, then quickly changed for dinner and headed for the formal dining room.

"I'm still full from lunch," Ashley confided as they sat down at the posh, linen-draped table bedecked with gleaming silver, crystal, and china.

"They must think I'm going to eat a horse," said Dixie, sitting down. "They've given me enough silverware for three people."

Ashley scanned the menu and smiled. "Don't worry, horse isn't even on the menu."

Dixie opened her menu. "Wow! Seven courses. Looks like we won't go hungry."

"Everything sounds wonderful. Shrimp cocktail, lobster, filet mignon, baked Alaska."

"Whoa! I'm definitely avoiding the caviar and snails."

After a sumptuous meal, they went to the theater for the Welcome Aboard show, featuring a juggler, a comedienne, and an Irish tenor singing show tunes. Afterward, they walked around the ship, visiting the gift shops, photo gallery, library, cinema, and spa.

"I love this spa." Dixie's gaze swept over a sculpted King Neptune surrounded by colorfully painted porpoises and graceful sea creatures. "I'm coming back here for a sauna, a lomilomi massage, and one of those Japanese silk facials."

"You mean where they put mud all over your face and cucumbers on your eyes?"

"Why not? I'll start a whole new fashion trend."

Ashley laughed. "Count me out. You go do your extreme makeover and I'll curl up with a good book in the library."

But there was hardly time to pick up a book, let alone read it. The weekend flew by—a steady stream of shipboard activities—shuffleboard, table tennis, golf lessons—and shore excursions to the Haleakala Crater and Eden Botanical Garden, with lunch at a Maui tropical plantation and snorkeling off a sixty-five-foot catamaran.

Ashley tried not to think about Ben. But she couldn't help herself. *It should be Ben and me standing here gazing at the sea at sunset. It should be Ben and me eating dinner over candlelight or strolling the deck at midnight.* No matter how much she threw herself into cruise activities, the ache in her heart never went away. At night, after Dixie fell asleep, Ashley slipped out onto her balcony and wept and prayed, prayed and wept, but she found little solace. Had God forgotten her? She had always felt His comfort before. Why not now?

On Monday morning Anthony Adler's lecture series began. There was a full-page write-up about him in the ship's daily newspaper.

Dixie scanned the article. "It says, 'Come hear world-renowned, best-selling author Anthony Adler talk about Hawaii's history and read from his novels on Hawaii.' We'd better get there early, Ash. The place may be packed."

"I'm coming." Ashley knew she was spending too much time applying her makeup and styling her long, honey-blond hair. Why did she care how she looked or what this man thought of her? As she slipped into her white capri pants and a stylish sea green blouse, she vowed not to worry about any man's opinion ever again.

"You look great. You're sure to impress Mr. Adler," Dixie told her as they walked to the conference room.

"I'm not trying to impress anyone," she countered, a bit too defensively.

The room was indeed packed. As they found seats in the next-to-last row, Ashley kicked herself for not coming early. What was wrong with her? She was dying to meet this man, and yet scared to death.

Anthony Adler was right on time. You couldn't miss him—a tanned, ruggedly handsome man with broad shoulders and curly black hair. He strode to the podium with the self-assured stride of a man who knew how to captivate a crowd. He was taller and more imposing than Ashley expected, with a brooding, roguish mystique she couldn't quite define. Perhaps it was the way his unruly locks tumbled over his high forehead or the way his heavy brows crouched over piercing, ice-blue eyes. He shuffled his papers, then smiled out at the crowd with a wry, controlled half smile.

"It's good to have you all here today," he said in a husky baritone. "You could have been onshore seeing Hawaii for yourself, but instead you chose to be here listening to me talk about Hawaii. I'm both flattered and humbled." He cleared his throat and looked down at his notes. "Hawaii became our fiftieth state in August 1959. The Aloha State, as it's called, lies 2,400 miles from the US mainland—the most isolated group of islands in the world and yet everyone's idea of paradise on earth."

Ashley's heart sank. *Don't tell me this is going to be a history or geography lesson. The man is obviously a better writer than speaker.*

Adler talked on about the Polynesian immigrants who settled in Hawaii over a thousand years ago, about Captain James Cook arriving in 1778, and about King Kamehameha uniting the islands in 1796.

I'm sorry, Mr. Adler, I've already studied Hawaii's history, she protested silently. *I know native Hawaiians are descendants of the Polynesians and represent one-eighth of the population. I know sugarcane and pineapples are Hawaii's most important crops and the tourist industry the most significant source of imported income. I don't want to hear facts and figures.* She had come to hear Mr. Adler read from his marvelous books and talk about how he had been inspired to write them. She sensed the crowd felt the same as she did. There was an undercurrent of whispers and shuffling feet, which ceased the moment Adler reached for one of his novels and began to read.

"At last!" Ashley sighed under her breath.

For the next hour the crowd was mesmerized as Adler talked about his books and his life, about how he had moved to Hawaii from the mainland when a Hollywood movie studio had filmed one of his novels in the lush, tropical beauty of Kauai's Waimea Canyon, the "Grand Canyon of the Pacific."

As Adler shared several personal anecdotes, Ashley found herself drawn to the man and unnerved by him all at once. Adler had put aside his notes now and loosened his tie. "My first editor told me to quit writing and paint fences or sell encyclopedias," he said with a hint of amusement. "He said I'd never be published. I took his words as a challenge. I vowed I would not give up until I had sold something to that man. It took me three years. He bought my first book, which was later made into that movie on Kauai."

The audience broke into spontaneous applause.

"The point is, don't give up your dreams," he concluded with a lilt in his voice and a twinkle in his eyes. "My advice to writers, to anyone, in fact, is live a passionate life. An inspired life. Have a passion for your work, whatever it is. Have a passion for people and a passion for God. Don't let a day go by without doing something that challenges you and stirs your passions. Life is too short. Time is a gift. And I thank you for giving me the gift of your time and attention today. I hope to see you all again tomorrow."

More applause. A standing ovation from some, including Ashley. As the audience filed out, she made her way to the podium. Adler was already autographing copies of his books for eager fans. She picked up a copy of his latest novel, even though she'd already read it, and handed it to him to sign.

"To whom?" he said without looking up.

"Ashley."

He scribbled something on the title page, then handed her the book.

He was already looking at the next person in line when she said abruptly, "Excuse me, Mr. Adler."

He looked at her for the first time. "Yes, miss?"

Her voice came out breathy and uneven. "I'm Ashley Bancroft, Ben's editorial assistant at Haricott."

Adler's brows shot up. "Oh, you're *that* Ashley!"

She nodded, taken aback. What did he mean by *that Ashley*?

"We've corresponded quite often over the past few years, haven't we? Even talked on the phone now and then. You've sent me my galleys and lots of corrections from Ben."

"I suppose I have."

"Wait a minute." He leaned forward, his vivid blue eyes locked on hers. "You and Ben were getting married and coming on this very cruise. He invited me to the wedding, but I was lecturing on a cruise ship in the Mediterranean at the time. Then I heard the wedding was canceled. And yet here you are. Does that mean you are Mrs. Bennett Radison after all?"

"No, I'm not. I'm still Ashley Bancroft." She felt the impatient stares of those waiting for their autographs. "I came on my honeymoon—I mean, it's not my honeymoon. It's just a cruise. I came on the cruise with my friend Dixie." She looked around, growing more flustered, only to spot Dixie standing off to one side, taking everything in. She gave Dixie an entreating glance: *Come get me out of this!*

Dixie sashayed right over and clasped Ashley's elbow. "We'd better hurry if we want to keep that appointment with the, uh, captain."

"The captain, eh?" said Adler, bemused. "You have an appointment with the captain?"

"N—not exactly," said Ashley. Why had she thought Dixie could bail her out? She was only making this moment more embarrassing.

Adler extended his hand. "Before you go, Miss Bancroft, would you like to have lunch sometime? Chat a little? You can catch me up on what's happening at Haricott Publishing."

"I'd love to," she blurted, then turned on her heel and rushed off with Dixie before Anthony Adler could say another word.

three

There was a phone message waiting for Ashley when she returned to her stateroom. It was Adler. "If you're still available for lunch, meet me at the Oceanview Café at noon. If you don't get this in time, perhaps we can talk tomorrow after my lecture. I trust you will be there."

"Well?" said Dixie. "You are going to meet him, aren't you?"

Ashley walked over to the sliding glass door, opened it, and stepped out onto the balcony.

Dixie followed her. "Did you hear me, girlfriend? This is your chance to get acquainted with the legendary Anthony Adler. Why would you even hesitate?"

"I'm not hesitating. I'm just feeling a little overwhelmed. He's so—so intimidating. And I feel so embarrassed about—you know—Ben leaving me at the altar. Mr. Adler must surely think I'm a loser with Ben walking out on me that way."

"Sure, and that's why he wants to have lunch with you."

"Don't make more of it than there is, Dixie. He just wants to find out what's happening at the publishing house."

"Whatever." They stood at the rail gazing out at the ocean—a sheer, sparkling span of cerulean blue. "Are you going to take your manuscript?"

"To lunch? Of course not."

"But you brought your novel all the way from New York because you wanted Adler's opinion of it."

"I do, but that would be rude of me to sit down and thrust my manuscript at him like a starry-eyed, unpublished novice."

"But isn't that what you are?"

"Yes, but I have my pride."

"Oh, well, that'll get you published for sure."

Ashley drummed her fingers on the polished cedar rail. "I already feel humiliated facing him, Dixie. I'm not going to dig myself in deeper."

"What's a little more humiliation if you get some expert help with your book? Imagine getting some direction from an author of his stature. That's to die for."

"I may do just that if he tells me I have no talent."

"Better to hear it from the best."

"Thanks. I thought you believed in me."

"I do, Ash. You're a terrific writer. But what do I know? I sell lipsticks and lotions. You need to hear it from someone who can encourage you and point you in the right direction."

"Well, Ben always said I have talent, but I was afraid he was prejudiced. I never had the courage to test the waters."

"We're sitting right here in the ocean. What better time to test the waters?"

By lunchtime, Dixie had convinced Ashley to take her manuscript with her to the Oceanview Café. She went with fear and trembling, her palms so moist, the thick manila envelope was damp. She held it behind her when she spotted Anthony Adler waiting by the café entrance. He strode over and greeted her with a beaming smile.

"I'm glad you could make it, Miss Bancroft. Or may I call you Ashley?"

"Please do, Mr. Adler." He looked as if he intended to shake her hand, but her hands were behind her, clutching her work.

"You may call me Tonio. All my friends do."

"Tonio?"

"It's a nickname that has stuck with me since childhood. My Italian grandmother called me Tonio."

"But Adler isn't Italian, is it?"

"No, I changed my name to Adler years ago. My birth name would be too long for most book covers. And no one could spell or remember it."

They made their way through the buffet line, then he carried both trays outside to a table near the pool. "Is this all right?"

"Perfect. The breeze feels great and the view is amazing." She set her manuscript at her feet. She shouldn't have brought it. No doubt Mr. Adler had noticed her balancing her tray on it in line.

He touched her hand. "May I ask a little blessing on the food?"

Surprise brightened her voice. "I'd love that."

He prayed a simple prayer, but it was enough to set her at ease and give her hope that Mr. Adler was a kind, approachable man after all. Perhaps he even shared her faith. "How are you enjoying the cruise?" she asked as they ate.

"Very nice. I've done several of these lecture cruises. The Mediterranean two weeks ago, as I mentioned. And Hawaii, naturally. Of course, I already live in Hawaii, but this gives me a chance to visit the other islands. I especially like the green, jagged mountains and soft white sand beaches in Oahu. You'll have to see—"

"Mr. Adler! Mr. Adler!"

A stout, middle-aged woman in shorts and halter top bustled over to the table with one of Adler's novels clutched to her chest. "Excuse me, Mr. Adler. It really is you, isn't it? I was just lying there on the lounge chair reading your book." She paused to catch her breath, her gaze taking in Ashley. "I'm sorry, I don't mean to interrupt, but I just love your work. I'm your greatest fan. Would you mind signing my book— *your* book—oh, you know what I mean. Make it out to Greta. Greta Morrissey, m-o-r-r-i-s-s-e-y."

Adler autographed the book and handed it back with a patient smile. Ashley watched as the woman returned to a cluster of people beside the pool, waving her prize.

"You must get that a lot—people chasing you down, wanting your autograph."

He sipped his iced tea. "It comes with the territory. People love having the chance to meet their favorite author. I figure they're my bread and butter. If I can make their day, why not?"

"That's a very generous attitude."

"What I don't like," he said in a confidential tone, "are those people who tell me a story and are convinced I'll want to write it. Of course, they're willing to share the millions we'll make when their story becomes a best seller and is made into a movie."

Ashley laughed in spite of herself. "I suppose everyone has a story."

"Yes. Everyone does. What's yours, Ashley?"

She gazed down at her plate. "Nothing special. I grew up in a little town in downstate New York and started working for Haricott right out of college three years ago."

"You enjoy editing?"

"Yes. But I prefer writing."

"Good for you. So do I. Writing is so much more fun than editing." His clear blue eyes crinkled with amusement. "That reminds me of another of my vexations—people who ask me to read their manuscripts and tell them whether they can write or not."

Ashley choked on her lemonade.

"Are you okay?"

"Yes, fine." She dabbed at her mouth with her napkin. "Does that happen often?"

"What?"

"People asking you to read their manuscripts."

"Oh, yes, all the time. Everywhere I go. They just assume I have all the time in the world. I'm afraid most of their so-called masterpieces belong in the recycle bin."

Ashley kicked her manuscript farther under her chair. "I can't imagine people being so brazen as to intrude on you that way."

"Nor can I. But it happens. Now, you're in the publishing business, so you know how exhausting editing can be. I would never presume to ask my dentist to stop by after work and clean my teeth, or ask my barber for a free shave."

"Of course not!"

Adler shrugged. "But people expect writers to always be on call. For example, if I were having lunch with some pleasant young lady I had just met—not you, of course—but some other attractive woman like yourself, I would hardly be finished with dessert before she would pull a sheaf of papers from her purse and ask me to have a look."

"You must be kidding."

"Not at all. Why, if I didn't know better, I would suppose that fat envelope you've been kicking around under the table was a novel or collection of stories you were hoping to show me."

Ashley's face flamed. "Oh, Tonio—Mr. Adler—I wouldn't!"

"Of course you would. I don't mind. You're not some rank amateur. You're in the business. Let me take a look." He reached down and grasped the envelope. "What is it—a novel?"

"Yes. Romantic suspense. It's only a first draft. Something I just threw together. Not very good, I'm afraid." She drew in a sharp breath and met his penetrating gaze. "Actually, it's my sixteenth draft." *And I poured my heart and soul into it. And if you say it's no good, I'll simply shrivel up and blow away!*

He pushed aside his tray, removed the hefty stack of bond paper and began reading. Ashley shifted in her chair, crossed her legs and uncrossed them, sipped her lemonade, and stole a glance at Adler. His expression was inscrutable. She looked around at the sunbathers, the tanned bodies frolicking in the pool, the glittering, sun-washed ocean—her gaze roaming everywhere, except in Adler's direction. Her heart was pounding so loudly, surely he could hear the terrified thumping. How could she have put herself in such an appalling situation—allowing the great Anthony Adler to read and criticize her work? It was her precious baby, after all, the fragile child of her soul. How could it survive his critical, merciless scrutiny? How could *she?*

He read for nearly ten minutes without saying a word.

His expression remained cryptic. Was he bored? Amused? Intrigued? The waiting was excruciating. Ashley inhaled sharply, desperate for more air. She couldn't decide where to rest her eyes. If she kept them focused on Adler, he might assume she was growing impatient. If she pretended to busy herself with her napkin or lemonade or a chipped fingernail, he might think she wasn't interested in his opinion. He had no idea that the world hinged this moment on the slightest arch of his brow or the curl of his lips.

After what seemed an eternity, he looked up at her. "May I take this back to my stateroom and finish reading it?"

"Of course." Her pride kept her from asking what he thought of it.

Surely he wouldn't make her coax him for a response.

He returned the pages to their envelope and stood up. "May I see you again, Ashley? Other than at my lectures?"

She stood up and gripped the table, her ankles weak. "Yes, I'd like that."

He tucked her manuscript under his arm. "Until tomorrow then."

She nodded, her mouth too dry to speak. As she watched him walk away, her spirits nose-dived. *What did you think of my novel, Mr. Anthony Adler? Did you love it? Hate it? How could you be so cruel as to leave me hanging this way?*

four

Tell me everything." Dixie was beside herself with questions when Ashley returned to their stateroom. "Is he as wonderful as he seems? Did he read your novel? Does he love it?"

"He didn't say."

"But you showed it to him?"

"Yes. He took it back to his room."

"That's a good thing, right?"

"I don't know if it's good or bad. He sat there reading my manuscript at lunch and never said a word. Never even cracked a smile or nodded his head. What have I done, Dixie? What if he thinks it's garbage and he's just trying to figure out how to let me down easy?"

"It's not garbage. It's good. I know that much. Just wait. He'll think so, too."

Ashley sank down on the sofa and crossed her arms on her chest. "I don't think I can face him again."

"Of course you can. You're going to tomorrow's lecture."

"I suppose. And he did ask if he could see me again."

Dixie's brown eyes brightened. "See you? As in a date?"

Ashley waved her hand dismissively. "Not a date. How could I even think of a date after losing Ben? Tonio and I are colleagues. Sort of. I'm sure he just wants to talk about the writing business."

"Is he married?"

"Stop it, little Miss Matchmaker. I've had enough of romance for a good, long time."

"Then he's not married?"

"He's a widower. His wife died about five years ago."

Dixie's voice softened. "Oh, I'm sorry. Me and my big mouth."

"I don't know much about it. It happened before I started working at Haricott. I heard he didn't write for nearly two years after her death. He must have loved her very much."

Dixie sat down beside her. "I wonder what happened. Usually the tabloids flash all kinds of headlines about famous people. But I don't recall hearing anything about Anthony Adler. Of course, I don't pay much attention to that sort of thing anyway."

"Nor do I. Even Ben, who's his friend as well as his editor, has never said a word about Tonio's personal life." Ashley absently twisted a strand of her hair. "But I do know one thing. Tonio's a very complex man. Compelling. Maybe even a bit eccentric."

"Maybe he's keeping a secret, something he doesn't want the world to know. Something tragic and unspeakable."

Ashley shook her head. "With your imagination, *you* should be the writer."

"Don't you see it, too, Ash? He's mysterious, mystifying. A man of secrets."

"He's a writer."

"So?"

"Let's face it, Dixie. By nature, writers are a little odd. We go around listening to voices in our heads. Sometimes our characters are more real than the people around us. We're a strange lot."

"You can say that again."

"And so are the people who befriend us."

Dixie made an exaggerated flourish. "*Moi?*"

"If the shoe fits. . ."

Dixie jumped up. "What time is it? I have an appointment at the spa for a hydrotherapy massage. Or is it an aromatherapy wrap and seaweed shower to detoxify and decongest my body systems? I forget which I signed up for."

"Are you sure you're not going to end up in some weird vegetable stew?"

"Are you kidding? I'm going to be gorgeous inside and out."

"Spare me the details."

Glancing in the mirror, Dixie fluffed her short auburn hair and checked her ruby red lipstick, then headed for the door. "I'll see you at dinner. Don't forget this is karaoke night. The Rendezvous Lounge at ten."

"I'm not singing."

"Then come cheer me on. It's my time to shine."

"Just don't sing those schmaltzy love songs that make me cry."

"I'm going to go with the eighties tonight. Don't worry, I'll stay away from the ballads."

Ashley smiled. "I'll bring my earplugs just in case."

That evening, against her better judgment, Ashley joined Dixie at the karaoke program. But her mind wasn't on the singing. She couldn't stop thinking about Ben. In her memory she replayed the events of their wedding; more accurately, the wedding that never was. She wondered what Ben was doing now, back in New York City without her. Did he pass by her empty desk at work and think of her? Did he miss her as much as she missed him? Did he regret calling off the wedding?

Halfway through the karaoke program, a strange thing happened. Instead of Ben's face, Ashley found herself picturing someone else's. She heard a different voice in her imagination. Not Ben's. Whose was it? Whose features was she tracing in her mind's eye?

The dreamlike image taking focus in her thoughts startled her.

Anthony Adler.

She pictured him giving his lecture, a bit stiff at first and then warming to the crowd. She traced his aquiline nose and the cut of his jaw as he sat reading her manuscript at lunch. She could hear his deep, resonant voice as he talked about a writer's passion.

Her face warmed with embarrassment. She had no business thinking of a man she had just met and hardly knew. Anthony Adler meant nothing to her. All right, he meant something.

She had admired him from afar. Not him; his talent. She dreamed of being able to write as well and producing novels that people loved to read. But that was it. She wasn't the sort of empty-headed girl to be starstruck or beguiled by someone famous.

Give yourself a break, Ashley. You're at a vulnerable place in your life since Ben left you at the altar. It's only natural you'd want to find someone else to think about. Sure, that was it. Her broken heart was grasping at straws, seeking a distraction. What harm was there in getting acquainted with a handsome, charismatic man like Anthony Adler, who also happened to be her favorite author?

And don't forget, he may be in his stateroom reading your novel at this very moment.

That thought alone unnerved her. What would he say to her at his lecture tomorrow? She could imagine him holding up her manuscript and telling the audience, "There's someone in this room who actually believes she can write well enough to be published. Listen to what this poor, deluded girl wrote."

Ashley clasped her hands over her ears. "No, please, I don't want to hear it!"

Dixie slipped into the seat next to her. "Wow, Ash, I didn't think my singing was that bad."

Ashley broke into laughter. "Not you, silly. It's—oh, never mind. Just my crazy imagination running wild again."

❧

The next morning, as Ashley entered the conference room, visions of Adler making fun of her novel lingered in her mind. She had almost decided not to come. But Dixie persuaded her, threatening to tell Adler why she was avoiding him. *She thinks you're going to read her book aloud and laugh at her.*

It was a silly, irrational fear; nothing to worry about. Ashley knew that. Something more was giving her misgivings about seeing Tonio again. *Tonio.* He had told her to call him that— the name his grandmother had given him. He said only his friends called him Tonio. Wasn't that a sign she was more to him than a face in the crowd?

But why would she want to be more?

Ashley mused over that idea—being more than a face in the crowd—as Adler greeted the audience and shuffled his notes. She tried to keep her mind on his lecture, but her thoughts meandered off to surprising places. She wanted to be sitting with Tonio at lunch again, chatting face-to-face, as if they were the only two people in the world. She wanted to hear him speaking in that caring, confidential tone, his gaze fixed only on her.

Maybe I'm just desperate to know what he thinks of my writing. It can't be anything else.

After his lecture, Anthony broke away from the crush of autograph seekers and called her name. "Ashley, wait a moment, please."

She glanced at Dixie.

"Go ahead, girlfriend. I'm running off to an ice-carving demonstration. I'm dying to find out what they do with those ice sculptures after they melt." She winked. "Just kidding. You and Mr. Hemingway have fun."

Ashley gave Dixie's arm a squeeze. "I'll catch up with you later."

"Let's hope he's crazy about your novel."

"If only!"

Ashley lingered near the podium while Adler signed his books and sent his jubilant fans on their way. As he stuffed his notes into his briefcase, she watched for a glimpse of her novel. It wasn't there.

"Would you like to have lunch together again?" His voice was buoyant, his eyes expectant.

"Yes, I'd like that."

They fell into step together, their arms touching as they walked. "Well, Ashley, we can eat again on the pool deck, or we can enjoy the formal luncheon in the dining room."

"Formal is fine." She grinned. "I'm actually getting used to linen and fine china and a dozen pieces of silverware."

"The trick is to start from the outside and work your way in."

"But what about the silverware at the top of the plate?"

He shrugged. "You've got me."

"Maybe the extras are for when you drop your fork and don't want to tell anybody."

"There you go. You've solved one of life's greatest mysteries." She smiled. "Just call me Sherlock."

Ashley's hopes of having Tonio to herself were dashed when the maître d' seated them at a table of ten. When the female guests realized a famous author was sitting at their table, they were abuzz with questions and lavish praise.

"I've been reading your books since I was a girl," said a woman who was obviously decades older than Adler.

"Thank you, ma'am." He kindly avoided pointing out that he was only in his midthirties.

"I loved your last book," said another. "But you never should have let Jasmine die. I cried for two days. I'll never forgive you for that."

"My apologies. I rather did like Jasmine myself."

"What are you writing now, Mr. Adler? Can you give us a little sneak preview?"

"I'm sorry, ladies," he said in his most benevolent voice. "I never discuss a work in progress."

"Oh, please, just a little hint?"

"Perhaps just a hint." Amusement played in his eyes. "But it must go no further than this table. It'll be our little secret. Agreed?"

With a flurry of excited exclamations, the women all agreed. In no time Tonio was on a roll, a showman at heart, thriving on the adulation of his fans. Ashley gave up any hope of having a private conversation about her novel.

After lunch, Tonio walked her to the grand foyer. "I'm sorry if the table conversation got a little carried away. I had hoped the two of us would have more time to talk."

"Me, too," she said, stifling her disappointment. "Maybe another time."

"Are you taking a tour of Kauai this afternoon?"

"Yes, Dixie and I are doing a tour of Kahili Falls."

"Are you going to play in Kauai's famous red mud?"

She laughed. "I don't know about the mud, but they say we'll be traveling along old sugarcane roads and through lots of buffalo grass."

"Well, in my opinion, the only way to see Kauai is by air." As he touched her arm, the sensation warmed her. "Would you like to join me after class tomorrow on a helicopter ride over Waimea Canyon? Your friend is welcome to join us, of course."

"Sounds like fun," she said, suppressing her eagerness. "I'll check with Dixie and let you know."

But Dixie begged off, explaining that she had made plans with several other passengers who also happened to be in the cosmetics business. Ashley didn't press the issue. She figured Dixie was giving her some alone time with Tonio in hopes of easing her heartache over Ben.

It turned out Dixie was right. Not that Ashley was about to forget Ben, but at least she was pleasantly distracted.

Over the next few days, she experienced some of the greatest adventures of her life. But as much as she enjoyed the tours, it was Anthony Adler who made the days special.

On their first sightseeing excursion, they rode the helicopter over the vast Waimea Canyon with its craggy, colorful peaks and lush green vegetation. "Mark Twain called this the 'Grand Canyon of the Pacific,'" Tonio told her as they gazed down nearly four thousand feet into the rugged canyon below.

She didn't have the courage to tell him she was afraid of heights. She gripped his hand so hard her knuckles turned white. But with him beside her she felt safe even as her stomach churned.

The next day the ship arrived at the Big Island and docked

at Hilo, a rustic, picturesque town with Victorian houses overlooking a half-moon bay. After a picnic dinner under the massive banyan trees, she and Tonio toured the summit of the Mauna Kea volcano, one of the world's highest mountains. "The ancient Hawaiians considered this the meeting place of heaven and earth," he told her as they watched a glorious sunset give way to a deep blue, star-studded sky.

"It's breathtaking," she agreed, meeting his gaze in the moonlight. But it was more than the scenery that stole her breath away. Anthony Adler was stirring her emotions in ways she hadn't expected to feel again, certainly not so soon after her breakup with Ben. *What's wrong with me?* she wondered. *Am I so fickle that I'm already attracted to another man?*

That evening the ship sailed to the western side of the Big Island and dropped anchor at Kailua-Kona, where Tonio lived. He insisted on showing Ashley and Dixie around his city, so early the next morning they took a tender ashore. Ashley was relieved to have Dixie along; maybe now her silly infatuation over Tonio would go away.

"This was once a major fishing community, but now it's considered the tourist and commercial center of the Kona Coast," he told them as they walked along the seawall and browsed nearby souvenir shops. "There's a lot to see and do here. We can go swimming, deep-sea fishing, snorkeling, kayaking, scuba diving, or, if you like, we can take an aerial expedition over the Big Island."

"If you mean a helicopter ride, this time I'll pass," said Ashley.

"Okay, we can do something that doesn't involve heights. How about a submarine or glass-bottom boat ride, if you're into tropical fish and coral reefs. Or if you're interested in the history of the island, we can visit the Captain Cook Monument, or Hawaii's first church, the Mokuaikaua, or the Ahuena Heiau temple where King Kamehameha died."

"I'm not much into dead kings," said Dixie. "Personally I

like to shop 'til I drop. But history's okay, too, as long as it's not too heavy."

"All right," said Tonio. "Maybe you'd like to visit the University of the Nations, where Christians from all over the world are trained for ministry."

"I'd love to," said Ashley.

"And you'll both probably want to see Pu'uhonua o Honaunau National Historical Park."

Dixie shook her head. "See it? I can't even say it!"

"It means 'Place of Refuge,'" said Tonio. "It's beautiful. I think you'd like it."

"Sounds good to me," said Ashley. "Let's start there."

The three of them packed the next two days with hiking, swimming, and sightseeing. They saw lava fields, volcanoes, black sand beaches, blowholes, sheer cliffs, and coffee farms. They visited historic churches, temples, and museums. And to placate Dixie, they stopped by every kiosk and souvenir shop on the island.

By the end of their second day in Kona, as they headed back to the ship, all three had to help carry Dixie's purchases— T-shirts that changed colors in the sun, floppy, wide-brimmed hats, enormous beach bags, flip-flops, sunglasses, plastic plumeria leis, and heavy cans of Kona coffee and macadamia nuts.

"You'll never get this all home on the plane," said Ashley, pulling a carved coconut monkey out of one sack.

"Sure I will," said Dixie. "I'll wear the shirts and hats and leis, and stuff everything else in the beach bags."

"I can see it now," said Ashley with a chuckle. "My best friend, the bag lady."

They all laughed, but the thought of flying home struck a wave of apprehension through Ashley's heart. *How will I face Ben again? What am I going to do with the rest of my life?*

five

On the last day of the cruise, questions about Ben and her future were still playing in Ashley's mind. It had been twenty-four days since he left her at the altar. Her weeks in Hawaii and on the cruise had given her a sweet reprieve from reality. But now it was time to return to a world that was painful and complicated. How would she face Ben again? Would she have the courage to quit her job? What was God's plan for her life?

Leaving the ship also meant leaving Tonio, a man she had grown to care about in such a short time. The thought of never seeing him again left an emptiness inside her. As much as it surprised her, she wasn't ready to let their friendship go.

Besides, they still had unfinished business. He hadn't once mentioned her manuscript—a fact that she had pushed to the back of her mind. Maybe he had forgotten it. Or perhaps he wanted to let her down gently. She had been foolhardy and naive even to show it to him. He was no doubt saving both of them an embarrassing moment. Whatever the case, a perverse sort of pride kept her from inquiring about it.

On their last evening together, as the *Sea Queen* docked again in Honolulu, Tonio invited her to dine with him in one of the ship's exclusive, reservations-only restaurants. They were seated at a candlelit table for two by a gleaming wall of windows overlooking the back of the ship. Tonio looked amazing in his tuxedo; he told her she was breathtaking in her jade-green satin gown. The sunset was resplendent. Violinists strolled from table to table, serenading the guests. The ambience was magical, the night filled with romance.

They ordered baked stuffed shrimp, poke salad with tamarind honey dressing, mahimahi sautéed with macadamia nuts, and crème brûlée. As usual, Tonio declined any alcoholic beverage; she appreciated that, as a fellow believer, he shared her conviction.

And she loved the way he reached across the table and took her hands when he asked for God's blessing on the food. His simple gestures of faith warmed her heart in a way she had never felt with Ben.

"What are you thinking, Ashley?" The candlelight danced in his blue eyes and accented his tanned, chiseled features. "You look so far away. I hope I'm not boring you."

"Of course not." She touched the back of her neck. "I was just thinking that this is our last night together."

"Don't remind me."

She lowered her gaze, searching for words. "You–you've been so kind to me. I don't know how to thank you. You've lifted my spirits and made this cruise one of the most memorable events of my life."

"No, Ashley, I should be the one to thank you." He leaned toward her as if he was about to share a secret. "I came on this cruise expecting to give my lectures, enjoy a few tours, and go home the same man I was when I came. But you've brought something special into my life. Something I don't want to lose."

Her face warmed as she murmured, "Nor do I, Tonio."

The waiter brought their appetizers then, so they lapsed into silence as they ate. They made only small talk as each course was presented. It was as if they had so much to say, but now that time was running out, they didn't know how to say it. When the waiter served dessert, Ashley held up a spoon from the top of her plate and said, "Now that the cruise is almost over, I finally know which silverware to use."

"You're ahead of me," said Tonio. "I prefer a simple knife, fork, and spoon."

When they had finished dessert, Tonio reached for something beside his chair. A manila envelope. How had Ashley not noticed?

❧

"I have something for you." He held out her manuscript.

She caught her breath. "I thought you had forgotten."

"No, I was waiting."

"Waiting for what?"

"Waiting to decide what I would say."

"Was it that bad?"

"No. That good."

"Really?" Her heart hammered in her chest. "You liked it?"

"Very much. You've created believable characters and placed them in some fascinating situations. You have a knack for dialogue and your plot is solid. I'm quite impressed."

Tears welled in her eyes. "When you didn't say anything, I thought you hated it."

"I loved it, Ashley. Naturally I made a few notations in the margins, just minor changes and suggestions."

"Of course. I appreciate any help you can give me."

He cleared his throat. "The truth is, I've been mulling something over for several days. I have a proposition for you."

"Proposition?"

"Wrong word. A proposal." He laughed. "For a writer, I'm having an awfully hard time expressing myself. What I'm trying to say is, I'd like to offer you a job."

"A job?" This conversation was getting more peculiar by the moment.

"I know you're reluctant to return to your position at Haricott Publishing."

She lowered her gaze. "I can't work alongside Ben anymore."

"That's why I think my proposition, uh, I mean, my job offer will solve both our problems."

"I don't understand. I know my problem is Ben. But what problem do you have?"

"I need an editorial assistant. Someone to do what you do at Haricott."

"You mean, edit manuscripts?"

"Yes. And someone to do research. A research assistant. Someone to help me prepare my next book for the publisher. I have a tight deadline and, as you know"—he smiled grimly—"my editor is a stern taskmaster."

She matched his smile. "Yes, Ben certainly is that, isn't he?"

"See? You know him so well—how he thinks, what he likes. You would be perfect for this job."

"I'm not so sure. You work at home, right? In Kona?"

"Yes. You would need to move to Hawaii. To my estate actually."

She felt suddenly shy. "You want me to live at your house?"

"Not exactly. I have a cottage behind the house. A very nice little place. It used to be the caretaker's cottage, but it's empty now. We could fix it up for you. Naturally, we want to avoid any impropriety."

"I appreciate that. The cottage sounds wonderful—that is, if I decide to take you up on your offer."

"Well, think about it, Ashley. Go back to New York and see how things are. If you feel comfortable staying at Haricott, I certainly understand. But if you find the situation intolerable and would like to test the waters, well, I would welcome you with. . ."

She sensed he was about to say "open arms."

"Uh, let's just say I would be very pleased to have you as my assistant. And there's no pressure. If you decide you don't like the job, or Hawaii, or me, or whatever, you're free to leave at any time—with a glowing job recommendation, of course."

"You say that before you even know my work?"

"I've read your work. And I know Ben would never have hired you if you weren't the best."

She turned the stem of her crystal water goblet between her fingers, her thoughts racing. *Lord, what do You want me to do? Is this Your answer for me? Help me to make the right decision.*

Tonio set his linen napkin on the table. "I can see I've overwhelmed you. Let's go out on the deck and get some fresh air. Don't give my offer another thought for now."

They both stood up. It surprised her how weak her knees felt. She gripped the table to steady herself. Tonio stepped over, put his hand at her waist, then led her out of the opulent restaurant to the open deck.

She welcomed the moist, salty breeze against her flushed cheeks. She and Tonio leaned against the mahogany railing, side by side, elbows touching. She inhaled deeply, wondering whether the past hour had been merely a dream. Had the great Anthony Adler actually asked her to be his assistant?

He looked down at her and smiled. She loved the way the moonlight played on his face. Softly he said, "Ashley, I hope I wasn't being presumptuous, asking you to quit your job and come work for me."

"No, Tonio. I'm flattered. And pleased. I want to say yes, I really do." She drew in a steadying breath. "I'm so tempted to say yes right now. But I need to pray about it. Everything in my life will change, and I need to know it's what God wants for me."

"I'll be praying, too. God willing, we'll be facing a fascinating future together. . .in the writing business."

She laughed lightly. "We'll show Ben Radison. We'll come up with a book that knocks his socks off."

Tonio clasped her hand. "That's the spirit! We'll knock him right off his feet."

They chatted for another hour or so, mostly small talk about the cruise and the quirky twists and turns of the publishing industry, with a few companionable silences tossed in. At last, he turned to face her. "I hate to see this evening end, but I do have some last-minute packing to do."

"So do I. They want our luggage outside our doors by midnight."

"That doesn't give us much time."

She sighed. "Not much at all."

They were silent as he walked her to her stateroom. He

paused at the door while she searched her satin bag for her room key. "Will I see you in the morning for breakfast?" he asked.

She put her key in the lock but didn't open the door. "Sure, I'd like that."

"What time does your plane take off tomorrow?"

"Dixie and I fly back to New York at one."

"I fly to Kona at noon."

They weren't alone in the long, elegant hallway, but, for Ashley, it seemed they were the only two people on earth. Tonio studied her for a long moment, his gaze unnerving. She felt awkward, unstrung, like a girl on her first date, reluctant to let her beloved go.

"May I give you a good-bye hug now?" he asked as he drew her into his arms. "Things will be crowded and hectic tomorrow."

Before she could utter a sound, he wrapped his arms around her. She loved the delicious warmth of his embrace.

"This isn't good-bye, Ashley," he whispered. "I'm counting on us being together again." He lowered his face to hers and brushed a kiss against her cheek.

Surprised, she turned her head, only to find his lips touching hers. They lingered a moment too long for the kiss to be accidental. Even after they had said good night, she still felt the sweet sensation of his lips on hers.

six

Hey, girlfriend," said Dixie, "do you have room in your suitcase for my coconut monkeys?"

Ashley stood in the doorway, gazing around her stateroom as if waking from a dream. Tonio's kiss had left her dazzled, distracted. She couldn't quite process the scene before her—Dixie surrounded by brimming suitcases and bulging beach bags. Their room looked like a souvenir shop with leis hanging on the closet door and hats and aloha shirts stacked on the desk.

Dixie plopped herself down on her suitcase and tried zipping it shut. "And I can't fit my conch shells in anywhere, Ash," she rushed on breathlessly. "Do you have an extra bag?"

"Maybe, maybe not."

Dixie stopped zipping and gave Ashley a long, hard look. "Are you okay? You sound weird. Like you're a million miles away."

"I am."

"You are what?"

"A million miles away."

"Now you're talking in riddles."

Ashley covered her cheeks with her hands. Her face felt warm, flushed. "You'll never believe what happened."

Dixie was listening intently now. "Tell me before you explode."

Ashley's words wafted on a sigh. "Tonio kissed me."

Dixie scrambled off the suitcase, took Ashley's hand, and led her over to the sofa. They sat down, facing each other. "He actually kissed you? Tell me everything."

"It was accidental."

"An accidental kiss? How does that work?"

"He didn't plan it. I didn't expect it. He kissed my cheek."

"Then it was just a friendly good-night kiss?"

"It started out that way. He surprised me and I turned my head. And then our lips were touching."

Dixie rubbed her hands together. "This is getting good. What happened next?"

"For a moment neither of us moved. We just stayed that way, our lips touching ever so lightly."

"And then?"

"And then he said good night and left." Ashley sat back and hugged her arms to her chest. "And now I don't know what to think or how to feel."

Dixie shrugged. "It doesn't really matter, does it? You live in New York, he lives in Hawaii. You'll be an ocean and a continent apart. You'll probably never see him again."

Ashley sat forward. "That's just it. I may see a lot more of him than I ever imagined. He asked me to come to Hawaii and be his editorial assistant."

Dixie's mouth dropped open. "Are you kidding me? Is this one of those reality shows where you try to shock your best friend with some wacky news flash? Come on, where are the hidden cameras?"

"I'm serious, Dixie." Ashley repeated the details of Tonio's offer, finishing with, "He really wants my help. He says, together we can come up with a novel that will totally amaze Ben."

"So that's it!"

"What?"

"This is about Ben. About making Ben jealous."

"No, it's not. I never even thought of that." Ashley stood up and strode over to her bed, away from Dixie's probing gaze. She took the chocolate mint from her pillow and tore off the wrapper. "It's a wonderful opportunity, Dixie. You know I can't go back to Haricott. I could never work with Ben again."

"Then you're going to accept Tonio's offer?"

She popped the mint into her mouth. "I told him I'd pray about it."

"But wouldn't you be, I don't know, jumping from the frying pan into the fire?"

"How so?"

"Ben just broke your heart. Are you going to risk that again with Tonio?"

"It's a business arrangement, Dixie. Not a romance."

"He kissed you. And you liked it."

Ashley closed her eyes and savored the melting chocolate on her tongue. There was no use trying to explain to Dixie what she herself didn't understand—her undeniable attraction to Tonio and the certainty that she had to pursue this wild-eyed adventure, no matter how crazy or irrational it seemed. Her heart had already decided. Unless God shut the door, she would be packing up her life and heading for Kailua-Kona and the beachfront estate of Anthony Adler.

※

Three weeks later Ashley boarded a plane for Hawaii. She had severed all ties with her former life—quit her job, moved out of her small, high-rise apartment, resigned from teaching her middle-school girls' Sunday school class, and said good-bye to family and friends.

As hard as it was leaving Dixie and her parents, she found it hardest of all to walk away from Ben. She kept reminding herself that he had left her at the altar, and yet a part of her kept saying, *If you stay in New York, maybe Ben will come to his senses and take you back. If you leave, you're ending all chances for a reconciliation.*

She had almost weakened when she stopped by the Haricott office to gather her belongings. Ben had wished her well and told her if she decided to come back, her job would be waiting for her.

Oh, Ben, don't you see? It's more than my job I want from you. Tell me you want me back, and I'll stay here forever.

But, of course, he said no such thing. Smiling politely, they exchanged pleasantries and were still flashing their pasted-on smiles when they said good-bye.

Now, a new, uncertain future lay before her—a lush, tropical paradise and the suave, sophisticated Anthony Adler. Ashley had no idea what to expect from either of them.

Tonio was waiting for her at the Kona airport. He greeted her with a circumspect hug, then collected her luggage and walked her out to his SUV. "How was your trip?" he asked as he opened the door and offered his hand.

She accepted his gallant gesture and climbed inside. "The flight was long. Lots of turbulence. And a two-hour delay in Honolulu."

"Well, you'll have a Hawaiian feast waiting for you at home."

She stared at him. "You cook, too? Is there no end to your talents?"

He laughed. "No, I don't even boil water except when I'm desperate for my coffee. Mika does all the cooking."

"Who?"

"Mika Kimura. She and her husband, Harry, work for me. She's my housekeeper; he's my gardener."

"Servants, no less! Don't tell me they live in the little cottage you told me about."

"They did for several years, but now they have a place of their own nearby. Mika arrives before breakfast and leaves after she's prepared dinner. They know that when I'm writing I'm a hermit at heart. A veritable recluse, I'm afraid. Mika acts as my unofficial secretary, fielding phone calls and keeping visitors at bay. She and Harry both know when to keep out of my way."

Ashley made a soft whistling sound. "I guess that's something I'm going to have to learn, too."

Tonio reached over and squeezed her hand. "That won't be necessary. You and I have many long hours of work ahead. I'm already behind deadline, so I'll be grateful for every hour we spend together." His voice took on a reassuring tone. "Not that I intend to be a slave driver, mind you. We'll take time to do all the touristy things I'm sure you'd like to do. I won't let you work yourself to death."

She managed a smile. "I'm glad of that." Privately, she wondered, *What am I getting myself into? Who is this man I've come halfway around the world to work for?*

They drove for about ten miles through lava fields that offered little of the beauty she had seen on the other islands. But minutes later, as Tonio headed up a winding, palm-lined road toward the cliffs, a glowing sun turned the sky burnt orange and cast fiery streamers on the ocean. She had never seen anything more breathtaking.

"We have a panoramic view here, Ashley. A little touch of heaven. I hope you love it as much as I do."

"I'm sure I will." Did she sound a bit hesitant? Did Tonio sense how self-conscious she felt?

In the distance she spotted a sprawling, plantation-style house perched on a rugged cliff. Tonio followed the circular drive around an expansive, manicured lawn to the front entrance with its wraparound porch flanked by towering palms. Bright orange birds-of-paradise stood like sentries among a colorful profusion of exotic flowers and plants.

"I'll show you around the grounds tomorrow," Tonio said as he unloaded her luggage. "The light will be better and you'll be rested."

"I look forward to it," she said, gathering up her purse, laptop, and cosmetics bag.

As they climbed the porch steps, he nodded toward the north. "Over there is a coconut grove and to the south, an avocado orchard. And if you walk far enough, you'll see acres of citrus, mango, and jacaranda trees."

"It's more beautiful than I imagined."

He showed her into an elegant entry hall with marble flooring and a grand teak spiral staircase. "Harry will take your luggage out to the cottage. I think you'll like it there. It's cozy and closer to the ocean. The main house has plenty of guest rooms, but as I said. . ."

"You're right. As a Christian, I wouldn't want to give anyone the wrong idea."

"Agreed. And by now Mika should have dinner ready for us."

"It smells wonderful. What is it? Spareribs?"

"You'll see. One of her pork dishes. You'll get a taste of authentic Hawaiian food."

"I can't wait."

She followed Tonio down a long hallway to the great room with its vaulted ceiling and teak paneling. The room was accented with mosaic tiles, etched glass, hanging plants, and tropical flowers. Leather sofas were grouped around a coffee table made of a mahogany tree trunk. At one end was a massive stone fireplace; at the other end French doors led into the dining room. But most spectacular was an entire wall of pocket sliding glass doors opening onto a covered lanai, blending inside and outside in a stunning vision of raw nature and unbridled opulence.

Ashley crossed the room and looked out at the sweeping view. "Oh, Tonio, it's amazing!" Tiki torches surrounded a huge swimming pool and spa. Beyond the pool lay a quaint cottage and Victorian gazebo framed against an orange and violet sky. Beyond the cottage, a rocky promontory led down to the turquoise splendor of the Pacific.

"I wish I were an artist," she told him. "I'd love to paint this scene."

"Paint it with words."

She smiled. "Maybe I will."

"Make yourself at home, Ashley. I'll check on dinner."

She pivoted, taking everything in. "Your home is gorgeous, Tonio. You have exquisite taste."

He raised his hand in protest. "Whoa. It's not me. None of this is me. I would have been happy in a little bungalow with inside plumbing and electricity."

"Then who designed and built all of this?"

He walked over by the French doors and gazed up at a framed portrait of a woman with remarkable beauty. "My wife," he said huskily.

Ashley's breath caught in her throat. This was the first time Tonio had mentioned his wife. And now, to see her in the vivid colors and swirling brush strokes of this oil painting was more than Ashley had bargained for. Suddenly she felt like a trespasser, barging into the privacy of a stranger's life.

"Brianna created this estate," Tonio said with a hint of irony. "She was born into wealth and inherited a fortune from her parents. That and my income allowed her to have everything she wanted—all these luxuries and amenities. She was relentless in her decorating, acquiring the best from all over the world— Italian marble, African mahogany cabinets, ceilings trimmed with monkeypod wood, Brazilian oak floors, and of course, lots of Hawaiian artifacts. She planned every detail, down to the native hardwood sculptures and glasswork."

"She did a fantastic job."

"Yes, she was a very talented woman." A long pause, then, "But she never lived to enjoy it."

Before Ashley could summon a proper reply, Tonio opened the French doors and called out, "Mika, we're here, and we're as hungry as bears."

A short, squat woman with ebony hair, round cheeks, and twinkling eyes bustled out and flashed a smile that lit up the entire room. "Aloha, Mr. Adler. Dinner is served."

Tonio nudged Ashley forward. "Mika, this is Ashley Bancroft, my new assistant. Ashley, this is Mika Kimura. She keeps my life running like a Swiss watch."

Mika beamed. "*Mahalo*, Mr. Adler." She reached out and clasped Ashley's hands between her calloused palms. "*Pehea `oe*, Miss Bancroft? How are you?"

"Fine, thank you, Mika."

"*Maika `i, mahalo.*"

Ashley looked at Tonio, as if to ask, *What did she say?*

He grinned. "She translated your words—'fine, thank you'—into Hawaiian. In no time she'll have you speaking the language like a native."

"I look forward to it, Mika."

They followed her into the dining room where the table was set for an island feast. Platters brimmed with barbecued pork ribs, sweet potatoes, fried rice, fresh pineapple, papayas, and passion fruit. Tonio pulled back Ashley's chair.

"Thank you. I mean, *mahalo*," she said, sitting down.

"You're welcome. You catch on quickly." He sat down across from her and held her hand as he asked the blessing. Then he passed her the ribs. "Mika wants to make a good impression on you."

Ashley speared several succulent ribs dripping with barbecue sauce. "Tell her she definitely did."

He passed her another dish that looked like purple paste. She eyed it skeptically. "What's this?"

"Poi. Made from the taro root. An acquired taste, I'm afraid."

"I'll try it." She scooped some onto her plate. "Why not? I have an adventurous spirit."

"You certainly do." He flashed a look she couldn't quite read, but it pleased her. "You've proved that, Ashley, by coming here."

She squared her shoulders and tasted the poi, then puckered her lips. "Maybe I'm not quite that adventurous yet."

"That's okay. You have lots of time to develop a taste for island cuisine."

She liked the sound of that. Lots of time for the two of them to get better acquainted. Lots of time to discover whether she had come here for more than a job.

They ate at a leisurely pace, and when they had had their fill, Mika brought out a tray of chocolate macadamia nut clusters, chocolate-covered ginger, and hot, black Kona coffee.

"You're spoiling me," Ashley protested. "If I keep eating like this, I'll rival the kalua pig in size."

Tonio laughed. "Never! You're perfect, Ashley. Graceful and lovely. Remarkable in every way."

Her face warmed with pleasure and embarrassment. She could think of nothing to say in return, so she focused her attention on her coffee cup. She sipped too quickly. The hot liquid made her face even warmer.

After dinner Tonio walked her out to the cottage—a rustic, charming little house with thatched roof, covered lanai, and bay windows, nestled among plumeria trees, lush ferns, and tropical flowers.

They crossed the lanai, and Tonio unlocked the door, then handed her the key. "Your luggage should already be inside. With jet lag and the time change, I'm sure you'll want to sleep in."

She nodded. "No alarm clocks for me."

"Mika will fix you breakfast whenever you're hungry. Just come on over to the main house when you're ready."

"Thanks. I feel like I could sleep for days." She laughed. "I'm kidding. I'll be ready to work tomorrow whenever you say."

They entered the cottage, Tonio leading the way and flipping on a light switch. "We'll play it by ear, Ashley. I want my assistant bright-eyed and bushy-tailed."

"I can't promise bushy-tailed."

"Okay. Perky then."

"Sorry. I don't do perky, either." Her gaze took in the wicker furniture, open-beamed ceiling, stone fireplace, and polished bamboo floors. Simple, unadorned, comfortable. She liked it. "But I promise to be alert and ready to work hard tomorrow."

"Can't ask for more than that."

He showed her around the cottage—the roomy living room with fresh-cut flowers and plants, a cozy kitchen with a bowl of fruit on the counter, and a pleasant bedroom with native art on the walls and a homemade quilt on the bed.

After a minute they walked back out to the living room

and he opened the door. "I'd better get out of here and let you settle in." He moved toward her ever so slightly, as if to offer a kiss or an embrace, then drew back suddenly and straightened his shoulders. "Sleep well, Ashley," he said. "I'll see you in the morning."

Then, without a backward glance, he was gone. Ashley was alone in her little cottage by the sea, a million miles away from everything and everyone familiar.

seven

Ashley woke to the sweet twitter of birds outside her window. She stretched leisurely, then rolled over and hugged her pillow. For a moment she couldn't remember where she was. New York? No. She opened her eyes and looked around.

Hawaii. Her little cottage by the sea. A little bit of heaven.

She climbed out of bed, padded barefoot to her tiny kitchen, and put on the teakettle. Surely there would be instant coffee in the cupboard. Or did Hawaiians drink only freshly brewed Kona coffee?

While she waited for the kettle to boil, she opened her wood slat blinds and gazed out the window at the shimmering ocean. *They say if you watch closely you can see whales and dolphins playing in the surf. Wouldn't it be sweet if I could phone Mom or Dixie and say I'm whale watching on my private lanai?*

She looked at the clock over the stove. Almost nine. She had overslept. No time for whale watching this morning. She'd better gulp down her coffee, throw on some clothes and a little makeup and head over to the main house. Tonio had told her to sleep in, but she wanted to make a good impression her first day on the job.

A half hour later she was on her way, passing the gazebo and swimming pool. A lean, deeply tanned man in straw hat and work clothes was trimming the hedge around the pool area. He looked up and grinned as she walked by. "Aloha, sistah."

"Excuse me?"

"You in da Aloha State, sistah. Everyone is family here."

"Oh, I see. Thank you."

"How you doin' dis fine mornin'?"

"Just fine. So you must be Mr. Kimura." She offered her

53

hand. "I'm Ashley. Glad to meet you."

He rubbed his hand on his overalls, then gingerly accepted hers. "You gon call me Harry. Dat's what dey all call me."

"Harry then. I suppose Mr. Adler is already well into his day."

"Ah. You gon find him in da office. But I tink he gon wait fo you fo breakfast."

"Oh, that's sweet of him. I'm looking forward to your wife's cooking. She fixed us a delicious meal last night."

"Ah, dat's some *ono kine grinds*. You know, some good food."

"It certainly is. Well, you have a good day, Harry. Aloha."

Ashley gave a little good-bye wave and hurried on to the main house. Mika was already setting Ashley's place at the table. After exchanging pleasantries, Ashley sat down and spread her linen napkin on her lap. Mika poured her a cup of steaming coffee then spooned a cheese omelet and Canadian bacon onto her plate.

"You like sweet bread French toast, Miss Bancroft?" Without waiting for a reply, Mika placed a crusty wedge beside the omelet.

Ashley stifled the impulse to tell her she rarely ate more for breakfast than a protein bar. "Thank you. It looks delicious, Mika."

A rustling sound behind her drew her attention. Tonio came striding into the dining room with a coffee cup in his hand. "Good morning, Ashley." He sat down across from her. "How did you sleep?"

"Like a log. I didn't hear a thing until the birds started chirping."

Mika brought the coffeepot over and refilled his cup. "You ready for your omelet, Mr. Adler?"

"Yes, Mika. With a little salsa and sour cream."

"You didn't have to wait for me, Tonio. You must be used to eating at the crack of dawn."

"Not quite that early. I didn't want you eating alone your first morning here."

"I'm not used to eating such big breakfasts. At this rate, I could end up a blimp."

"A very nice blimp, I'm sure."

She chuckled. "You're no help, Tonio."

He winked. "Don't worry, I'll keep you so busy you'll burn every last calorie."

After breakfast, Tonio showed her to his office—a large, teak-paneled room with mahogany furniture, an entire wall of books, and floor-to-ceiling windows that faced the sea.

"Sweet!" she said. "I could get used to working in a place like this."

He pulled back a chair for her at the massive desk. "I'm counting on that."

She sat down, her gaze sweeping the dictionaries, research books, used coffee cups, and stacks of manuscript pages and unopened mail surrounding the computer. One thing for sure, Tonio was no neat freak.

"You can see I need some help," he said, sitting down beside her.

"It looks like you need a secretary." She picked up a handful of letters. "Is this fan mail?"

He nodded. "I have several stock reply letters on the computer, but it still takes time to read the letters and decide which reply to send."

"So that will be my job?"

"A small part. Mainly I need help with my current writing project."

"What do you want me to do? Research? I'm pretty good at that."

"Yes, research. And editing. I know you did a terrific job for Ben."

"Yes, but I wasn't editing *his* writing. Most authors are so protective of their 'literary babies,' they dread an editor red-penciling their work."

"I'm not like that, Ashley. I know I tell a good story, but

I'm not into the details. Right now I need someone with a discerning eye, someone who can keep me focused and on track, someone who can keep me accountable and moving ahead."

She pursed her lips slightly, wondering, *What am I getting into?* "I hope I can live up to your expectations."

"You will. I feel it in my bones."

"So where do we start?"

He handed her a loose-leaf notebook. "Here's the synopsis of my current novel. You'll find the plot outline, plus detailed sketches of all the main characters. I'm well into the book, but the deadline was last month. Ben has given me an extension, but it's still going to require a rigorous writing schedule over the next few months."

"You're not the only writer who's had to ask for more time, Tonio. It happens all the time. Authors sign contracts with a certain deadline, but then life intrudes. Sometimes it can't be helped."

Tonio cracked his knuckles. "This was totally my fault. You probably already know my last novel didn't do as well as my previous ones. Haricott is putting the pressure on. Not Ben. It's not editorial; it's the marketing division. They said they won't be putting as much promotion and advertising into this one unless the advance sales are high."

She gave him a sympathetic smile. "It's a recipe for trouble when a writer starts focusing more on marketing and sales than exploring the lives of his characters."

"Well said. See? You're already helping me put things in perspective. Let's get into these characters and see what we can do with them."

Ashley flipped through the notebook, scanning the plot points and character sketches. "I'll read through this later. For now, just tell me in your own words what the book's about."

He sat back in his chair and tented his fingers. "It's the story of a man—Philip Holt—whose wife is murdered. Holt has been a roustabout, a jack-of-all-trades, doing undercover work for the FBI and CIA, but that's all behind him now. He messed up, and now he's out on his own, doing small-time detective work. But his life is consumed with finding out why his wife was killed. What did she know or what did she have that made someone want her dead? And will that someone want him dead, too? So his mission in life is to track down his wife's killer. His motives aren't merely rational; they're emotional. He wants justice for his wife and revenge for himself."

"I like it," said Ashley. "It's bursting with tension, conflict, and emotion. A story like that should practically write itself."

He smiled grimly. "You'd think so. But it's not happening. I'm dead in the water."

"Well, let me read what you've written. Everyone faces writer's block at one time or another. Maybe you just need a little push to get you over the next hurdle."

He handed her the stack of manuscript pages. "Be my guest."

They spent the rest of the day working, reading, dissecting the story line, and batting ideas back and forth about the characters' motivations. Mika slipped in sometime around noon to bring them ham sandwiches and iced tea, but they continued discussing the novel as they ate.

Later, as Tonio set their empty plates aside, he said, "We should have taken an actual lunch break, Ashley. I apologize."

"No, I don't mind. We're on a roll. I'm used to eating while working."

"I promise you a leisurely dinner and maybe a movie on the DVR tonight."

"That sounds pretty tempting. But I'd rather spend the evening reading what you've written so far, so I'll be up to speed tomorrow."

"All right. We'll save the movie for another night."

Ashley stayed up until after midnight reading Tonio's work. The next morning she gave him her opinions. The writing was solid, the story line complex and captivating, the characters well drawn. "But there's a problem with Philip, your main character."

"Not macho enough?" said Tonio playfully.

"No, he's plenty macho. But I never felt like I really got into his head. There's all this action, but it all seemed to be happening from a distance. I wasn't living it inside Philip's skin. You didn't make me care enough about him. He's just a guy with troubles. Big troubles, sure. But he could be any guy."

"Okay, that's a valid criticism. What do we do about it?"

She shrugged. "You tell me."

"I have an idea. Let's make a game of it. Why don't you try your hand at writing a few scenes? I'll do the same and we'll compare notes."

"Sounds interesting. And a little intimidating. I'm not sure I want to be comparing my writing to a pro's."

"Aw, come on. It'll be good experience for you. And it'll help me see my work with fresh eyes, another point of view."

"Okay, you're on." She held out her hand. He shook it and didn't let go until she withdrew it. "I guess we'll have to put off that movie for another night," she told him. "Looks like tonight we'll both be busy writing."

Tonio glanced at his watch. "Actually, I won't be home tonight. I have an appointment in town."

"Oh? Do you want company?" The question had slipped out before she realized how forward it sounded.

"Not tonight, Ashley." There was something troubling in his voice. "This is something I have to do alone."

His sudden sternness flustered her. "I'm sorry. I wasn't trying to impose on your plans. I'll spend the night curled up with my laptop."

His tone softened. "Any other time I'd love to take you into town and show you the sights. It's just not possible tonight."

"I understand. You don't owe me any explanation."

After dinner that evening, Tonio excused himself and left the house with only a brisk good-bye. *Maybe he has a date and was afraid of hurting my feelings,* Ashley mused as she walked back to the cottage alone. *I'm only his assistant. I have no right to be concerned about what he does or where he goes or who he's with.*

Ashley spent the night writing. She became so engrossed in the story line, she forgot about Tonio until she heard his SUV in the driveway. It was after ten o'clock. *He won't have any time to write tonight,* she mused.

Sure enough, the next morning, when she showed him the three scenes she had written, Tonio admitted he hadn't completed his part of the assignment. "I'll write twice as much tonight," he promised. After reading her work, he sat back and whistled through his teeth. "This is amazing, Ashley. This is even better than what I read of your novel on the cruise."

"Really?" Her stomach fluttered. Was the great Anthony Adler actually raving about her work?

"You've got to do more. These scenes are riveting. Let your imagination go. See what else you can do."

"Okay. I'll try a few more scenes."

The next day she delivered a dozen more freshly written pages. Tonio was effusive in his praise. "These are excellent. You *will* be published, Ashley. It's not a matter of *if.* It's *when.*"

Like a schoolgirl receiving an award, Ashley basked in his approval. She had waited all of her life for moments like these. "I'm blown away, Tonio. I was so afraid you wouldn't like my work."

"Like it? I love it!"

"Now it's your turn," she ventured. "What did you write?"

He waved his hand. "Nothing like this. A few scribblings. They're rough. You'll see them after I've polished them."

The days took on a predictable routine. She showed him what she had written, and he lavished her with praise. But he somehow avoided showing her his work, saying it wasn't suitable yet for an editor's eye.

On Sunday morning, he took her to a quaint, open-air church where a worship band accompanied the congregation as they sang praise songs. Ashley loved the pastor's simple, heartfelt message and the friendliness of the people.

After church he drove her around town, showing her the sights. They spent hours browsing the art galleries of Holualoa, a quaint artists' community on the hill above town. They had dinner at a charming little restaurant on the boardwalk just past the seawall on Ali'i Drive. They ordered green salads with sesame-ginger dressing, bow tie pasta with scallops and shrimp, and finished with pineapple sorbet for dessert, all the while watching a ripe orange sun set over the cruise ships in the harbor.

On Monday they went back to work on Tonio's novel. She wrote more scenes and sketched out ideas for future chapters. And he gave more excuses for not showing her his writing.

The days slipped by in a seamless routine, one that was becoming more troubling to Ashley. It seemed that Tonio was going out almost every other night, with never a word about his destination. Whenever she inquired about his mysterious appointments, he changed the subject. Even Mika seemed closemouthed on the subject. "Mr. Adler is a busy man. He has important things to do. Very busy."

But I'm his assistant, she protested silently. *Shouldn't he take me into his confidence?*

One night Ashley's frustration came to a head. Tonio had gone out for another of his mysterious meetings, leaving her at home alone to write. As much as she enjoyed sharing her creative efforts with Tonio and receiving his feedback, she had come here to edit *his* work. But how could she edit what he refused to let her read? And how could he write when he was gone so much?

It wasn't just Tonio's capricious behavior that bothered Ashley tonight. She was feeling lonely and homesick. She missed everyone back in New York. Her parents. Dixie. And Ben. From time to time Ben would phone for an update on Tonio's novel. She always tried to remain detached when she heard his voice, but all her resolve melted when he said her name.

Making things even more complicated were her growing feelings for Tonio. How could she be having romantic feelings for him when she still loved Ben? And why did she allow herself to care for Tonio when he was her employer, nothing more? Actually, he was more. He was her friend. *Just a friend,* she realized with a ripple of disappointment. There hadn't been a hint of romance since their last night on the cruise.

At about ten o'clock Ashley closed her laptop and reached for her Bible. She needed some alone time with God. She read for a while, but the air was too warm and muggy to concentrate. She went out to her screened lanai and stretched out on the lounge chair. She needed to pray, but she felt empty of words tonight. "Lord, my feelings are so jumbled, I don't even know what to say. So maybe I'll just sit here in the darkness and listen for Your voice in the breaking surf."

She closed her eyes, letting the rhythmic roar of the waves relax the taut muscles in her arms and legs.

Sometime later—was it minutes or hours?—Ashley woke with a start. Every nerve in her body bristled. Had she been asleep? What had wakened her? She held her breath, listening.

Then she heard it. The rustling sound of footsteps, someone walking near the gazebo. Was it a prowler? Until now it hadn't occurred to her how vulnerable she was—a young woman alone at night on a flimsily screened lanai.

She slipped off the lounge chair and looked out toward the pool. A shadow loomed near the hedge. She couldn't be sure, but it looked like Tonio. She started to call out to him, then thought better of the idea. He was a man who cherished his privacy. If he wanted to be alone, she wasn't about to intrude. But why was he out roaming around his property in the middle of the night?

Ashley's curiosity got the best of her. If Tonio was out walking around this hour, she was going to find out why. She put on her sandals, quietly opened the lanai door, and walked through the pool area to the surrounding hedge. No sign of anyone. She looked beyond the hedge to the woods that led to the promontory above Tonio's estate. Was that someone moving through the citrus and jacaranda trees? She couldn't be sure. Maybe it was just a gentle wind coming off the ocean, rustling the trees.

No, it's Tonio. I know it is. Something's going on. I've got to find out what.

She crossed the lawn and made her way through the dark wilderness of trees. The air was heavy with the muggy scents of earth and tropical foliage. With the thick overhang of branches, she no longer had a bright full moon to show the way. She stumbled on a gnarled root and nearly fell, but her hands caught hold of the tree's rough bark. She steadied herself and caught her breath.

What if it's not Tonio? What am I doing wandering through a forest alone at this time of night? I must be insane.

Just as she considered turning around and going back, she came to a clearing at the edge of the cliff. The moon lit the way again, and what she saw took her breath away. Tonio stood on the rocky ledge gazing down into the wind-tossed sea. She stopped dead in her tracks, not moving a muscle, lest he hear her, turn, and lose his footing. She wanted to cry out, *Tonio! Get back before you fall!* But something in his stance kept her silent. Was he thinking of jumping? Surely not. And yet, why had he come here in secret in the dead of night?

After a minute he stepped back from the edge and knelt down beside something in a neatly manicured patch of grass. From her vantage point, Ashley couldn't see the object of his attention. *Please, Lord, don't let him discover me here. He would never forgive me for violating his privacy this way.*

He remained in a kneeling position for several minutes, so long that Ashley's legs went numb from standing so still in the shadows. She sighed with relief when he finally straightened his torso, flexed his shoulders, and strode off through the woods back toward his estate.

She waited until she was sure he had time to get back to the main house. Then she stole out of the shadows and made her way over to the object in the grass that Tonio had found so riveting. Reeling with shock, she stared down at a sculpted angel glistening in the moonlight. The angel was holding an urn. The base of the sculpture bore the inscription:

IN MEMORY OF BRIANNA ADLER
BELOVED WIFE
JUNE 22, 1973 – SEPTEMBER 17, 2003

eight

Tonio is still in love with his dead wife. He must be. He made a memorial to her on the cliff. Her ashes may even be in that urn. He's still totally devoted to her. He'll never have a place in his heart for another woman.

Those were Ashley's thoughts as she darted through the woods back to her cottage. How could she have been so foolish as to let herself become emotionally involved with a man she hardly knew, an eccentric, reclusive man with so many secrets?

It was nearly three a.m. when she finally climbed into bed. But she couldn't sleep. She was heartsick, imagining Tonio still carrying his grief around like an iron shield over his heart. There was no way a mere woman could penetrate that kind of pain. No wonder Tonio was having a difficult time writing. He was too bound by his sorrow to tap into his creativity. Why hadn't she seen that before? No wonder he made no romantic overtures. That kiss on the ship had been an accident, an aberration, a fluke. He had made sure it never happened again. If he ever suspected she had a crush on him, he would no doubt be mortified.

I've got to focus on the reason I came here. I'm his assistant. I'm here to help him get his book written. I'm going to edit his work, whether he feels the material is ready or not.

She fell asleep at last with a new resolve to accomplish the job she had been hired to do. Maybe her time on the island would be shorter than she had planned. Maybe in a month or two she would return home to New York and start a new life for herself.

The next morning, Tonio was late coming to the office, so

Ashley lingered in the great room with a second cup of coffee. She was drawn to the portrait of Brianna Adler on the wall by the French doors. As she studied the exquisite face and striking green eyes, she felt as if Brianna were speaking to her from the grave. *You have no business in my home. You're an intruder. Get out, and let Tonio grieve in peace!*

She shivered. The words weren't audible, and yet they thundered in her mind like a death knell.

"Well, you look deep in thought."

She whirled around. "Tonio, I didn't hear you come in."

"I apologize for being so late. Would you believe, I forgot to set my alarm." He managed a grim smile. "The truth is, I didn't sleep very well last night."

"I know. Uh, that is, I know what you mean." She pushed back a stray wisp of hair. Had he guessed she was there at the cliff last night? "Neither did I. Sleep well, I mean."

"Then we'll have to make an early day of it and get our rest tonight."

"No argument from me."

He walked her to the office and they sat down at his desk. He reached for a stack of letters. "Let me go through some of this mail. Then we can buckle down and get some work done on the novel."

She turned on the computer. "You know, I think I forgot to back up yesterday's work." She scrolled down through several files, copying them to the flash drive, until she came to one she didn't recognize. "That's strange. This wasn't here yesterday."

Tonio set down his letters. "What wasn't there?"

"This file. 'Material for Ben.'"

"It's nothing. Just ignore it."

"But if it's for Ben, it must be important."

"I said ignore it, Ashley. I changed my mind. I'm not sending it."

"Why? Because you don't think it's good enough?"

"I didn't say that." His tone sharpened. "Just let it go, Ashley."

"I can't, Tonio. Ben has been wanting to see something for weeks." She clicked on the file. "Let me read it, and if I think it's good enough, I'm going to e-mail it to him."

"Don't!" Tonio reached over and seized her hand that held the mouse. "I don't want you reading that."

But her eyes were already scanning the words on the screen. "I don't understand." She scrolled down several pages, reading the all-to-familiar lines. Her stomach knotted. "These are the scenes I wrote. Why would you be sending them to Ben?"

Tonio's hand tightened on hers. He looked away. "I was feeling lousy last night. I knew Ben was getting impatient. I read over your scenes again. They could have been my words. They said exactly what I wanted to say."

"You were going to send my work to Ben?"

"I considered it, for all of a minute."

"You mean you were going to pass my scenes off as yours? That's plagiarism! How could you even think of such a thing?"

Tonio put his head in his hands. "I never would have done it, Ashley. But the fact that it even occurred to me scares me senseless. I was dead wrong. I was feeling so desperate that for a brief moment it seemed like a solution. I knew as soon as I copied the file that I was on a slippery slope. I wrote Ben a note at the end of the file. Scroll down and read it."

Ashley went to the end of the file and scanned the brief note.

> *Ben, I wish I could say I had written these scenes, but I didn't. Ashley wrote them. What would you think of letting her coauthor this book with me? Just a thought.*
>
> *Tonio*

She looked up at him. "I don't understand you, Tonio. First you consider plagiarizing my work. And now you want me to be your coauthor?"

"No. I realized that was a cop-out, too. That's why I didn't send the e-mail to Ben. I realized I have to do this myself, on my own, with God's help, of course, if He'll forgive me for almost yielding to a very serious temptation."

"He will, Tonio, if you're truly sorry."

"I am. I've always considered myself a man of honor. I pray God will help me to live up to those words. And I pray He'll help me work through this dry spell."

She touched his arm. "You're the real thing, a genuine novelist with his own voice and style and message. You don't need to hide behind anyone else's writing. Certainly not mine."

He sat forward and lowered his gaze, his jaw tightening. They fell into an uneasy silence. He massaged his knuckles, cracking one, then another.

He looked at her, his brows furrowing. "Have I lost your trust, Ashley?"

"Why would you say that?"

"I can see it in your eyes."

"I want to trust you. I need to trust you, Tonio. I could never work for someone I had doubts about."

"So you admit you have doubts?"

"No. You're twisting my words."

"Am I?"

"It's just that the truth is very important to me. If people aren't honest with each other, what do they have?" A thought came unbidden: *What about you, Ashley? Are you going to tell him you were on the cliff watching him last night at his wife's grave?* She pushed the thought away. "I do trust you, but the truth is, we still don't know each other very well. We both have a lot to learn."

He stood up and walked over to the windows, his back to her. "One thing you'll learn very quickly, Ashley. I'm a very private person. I don't share my feelings easily. Maybe that's why I write fiction. That's the only way I'm able to get my feelings out. I pour them into the lives of my characters and let them deal with the fallout."

She nodded. "I think all novelists do that to some extent. I know I do. I'm probably saying this badly, so forgive me, but. . ." She paused, searching for the right words. "The truth is, I don't see those emotions in your current book. Maybe that's why you're struggling with writer's block."

He pivoted and returned to his desk. "Okay, I've admitted I'm having a dry spell. But who says I'm struggling with writer's block?"

"Aren't you?"

He sat down and spread his elbows over the padded arms of his chair. "You've got me there. So you want the truth?" He handed her his notebook. "Look at the tripe I've produced over the past few weeks. It's all garbage, junk I would have thrown out if even a beginning student had turned it in to me."

She thumbed through the notebook for several minutes. "It's not bad, Tonio. A lot of research. Some well-developed plot points. But—okay, I'm being honest now—I don't see the heart of your story here. It's what I said before. You've got to let me into your main character's heart and head. Your reader has to feel he knows Philip Holt as well as he knows himself."

"What you're saying is, I've got to open an artery and let it bleed all over the page."

She nodded. "Something like that."

"Any suggestions?"

"Maybe. If you're willing to listen objectively and not argue with me until I'm finished."

A smile played at the corner of his mouth. "You're asking a lot, lady."

"There's a lot at stake."

"Agreed. So what are your ideas?"

She picked up a pencil and tapped it on the desk. "Give me a minute to gather my thoughts, okay?"

He stood up. "Take your time. I'll get us some fresh coffee."

When he returned with the coffee, she was already jotting down notes. She set down her pencil, accepted the cup, and sipped the hot liquid. *Lord, give me the right words,* she prayed silently.

She moved her chair closer to his and placed his notebook on the desk so they could both read it. "Look at your story line. You have Philip giving up his entire life to find and get revenge on his wife's murderer."

"Right. And I think it's a solid story."

"It is. We agree on that. But you're still holding Philip's feelings back from the reader. You've made Philip clever and strong, like an iron man, a Superman doing incredible feats of bravery."

"That's what my readers like."

"Of course they do. But I think they want more."

Tonio shrugged, as if to say, *What more do they want?*

She lifted her chin decisively. "They want to see Philip's soul."

He drummed his fingers on the desktop. "This isn't some melodramatic romance novel, with emotions dripping on every page."

She bristled. "There's nothing melodramatic about portraying a character's emotions, whether it's women's fiction or a mainstream novel like this."

"You're right. I'm sorry. I spoke out of turn."

"Apology accepted."

A hint of defiance edged Tonio's voice. "So tell me what Philip is missing, and I'll do my best to correct it."

Ashley hesitated. How could she separate Philip, the fictional character, from Tonio, the flesh and blood man? Neither was successful in expressing his grief. How could Tonio tap into his character's pain when he was so desperately hiding his own?

Lord, I've got to say this carefully. I don't want to offend Tonio. I don't want him to feel I'm trespassing on his private life. Help me to keep this just about his book.

"Ashley, did you hear me? Tell me the problem as you see it."

She drew in a sharp breath. "Okay. Here goes. The problem is we don't feel Philip's anguish over losing his wife. Your readers have lost loved ones, too. They want to know what Philip is experiencing—the pain, the regrets, the struggles—and they want to know how he copes with his grief, and how his grief makes him stronger. You do a wonderful job of portraying the physical action of your story, but you ignore what Philip is going through on the inside. Do you see what I mean?"

Tonio rubbed his chin thoughtfully. "If you're suggesting I dump my private torments onto my readers, I must deny your request. They don't deserve that, and neither do I."

"That's not what I'm saying. I'm not suggesting you expose your personal life to your readers."

"Really? It sounds like that's exactly what you're saying."

Tears welled in her eyes. *Oh, no, Lord, don't let me start crying like a silly schoolgirl!* "I'm just saying—I know you've been through a terrible loss—I know you don't want to talk about it. Maybe you think it's a sign of weakness to admit you're hurting—I don't know—I just know your novel will be stronger if you let yourself explore your feelings about your wife's death and if you bring those feelings to your characters. That's all I'm saying."

Tonio said nothing.

Before succumbing to a deluge of tears, she bolted out of the chair and hurried from Tonio's office, slamming the door behind her. She ran back to her cottage, threw herself on the bed, and let the tears flow. What was wrong with her, that her emotions were suddenly so ragged? Was she crying for Tonio, or for herself? Or both?

After awhile, she got up and washed off the mascara from around her eyes. "Ashley Bancroft, you look like a raccoon," she muttered to her reflection. She went back to her room, sat down on the bed, and picked up her Bible. "Lord, I was so shaken that Tonio would even consider passing off my material as his. Thank You for delivering him from that evil. Help him to find the breakthrough he needs in his writing. I know he's hurting, and I don't know how to help him. In fact, I'm afraid I've really made a mess of things. He probably hates me now for poking my nose where it doesn't belong. I can't fight what he feels for his wife. I can't make his pain go away. Only You can do that."

After freshening her makeup, she went back to the main house. She dreaded facing Tonio after her unceremonious departure. But she had a job to do, no matter how embarrassed she felt.

It was lunchtime and Mika was serving coleslaw, fish sandwiches, and chips in the dining room. Ashley took her place at the table and placed her linen napkin on her lap. It was all she could do to meet Tonio's inquiring gaze. "I'm sorry," she mumbled. "I don't know why I ran out like that."

"No problem. The conversation was getting a little intense. We'll start fresh after lunch. I promise to keep things peaceful and pleasant."

"Me, too."

When they returned to the office, Tonio was carrying a plate of freshly baked macadamia nut cookies. "These will give us a much needed pick-me-up when the conversation gets too heavy," he said with a bemused wink. "No one can have a sour expression on their face when they're eating one of Mika's cookies."

Ashley sat down at the desk and folded her hands on her lap. "Well, just so you know, I plan to keep my opinions to myself from now on. I'm your employee. I have no right meddling in your personal life."

Tonio gave her shoulder a brief squeeze as he sat down beside her. "You had every right to speak up, Ashley. You're more than an employee. You're a friend. I've been alone for so long, I don't always say the right thing. When it comes to being sensitive to other people's feelings, I'm sometimes like a bull in a china shop. I feel like a jerk for making you run out of here in tears."

"You didn't. I don't know why I got so emotional. It's just that I care so much about, um, your book." She bit her lower lip. She had almost said, *You. I care so much about you!*

He grinned. "That's what I love about you, Ashley. You care

about this cumbersome pile of manuscript pages almost as much as I do."

She met his gaze. "Yes, I do. So maybe it's time to get to work."

He put his hands on the keyboard. "I'm going to do what you suggested. I'm going to explore Philip's emotions about his wife."

"Wonderful! What can I do to help?"

"Continue your research on some of the topics I'll be covering. And remind me to come up for air every once in a while. This could get pretty deep."

She stifled a laugh. "Just let me know and I'll send out a rescue crew." She reached over and touched his wrist. "One more thing."

"Yes?" His blue eyes twinkled.

"When I write, I always pray first for God's guidance. He's the Author of all creativity and my partner in writing, so I want every word to be blessed by Him."

Tonio nodded. "Don't know why I didn't think of that. We ask God to bless our food. Why not our words?"

"Would you like to do the honors?" she asked.

"No, you go ahead. I have a feeling God really listens to your prayers."

"He hears yours, too."

Tonio turned his eyes to the keyboard. "I know He does. And I do pray. But the truth is, it's been awhile since I felt really close to God."

Ashley swallowed hard. Tonio had just delivered a zinger with hardly the bat of an eye. She had considered him a devout man. Was he saying his faith was superficial? Was he just going through the motions? He was waiting for her to pray, so she bowed her head and said the appropriate words, but her mind was spinning with questions. *What is Tonio really like? Who is he in his heart of hearts? Every time I think I'm getting to know him, he does something to throw me off. Have I even begun to know the real man?*

nine

Tonio spent the next three days writing furiously. Ashley busied herself with research and answering fan mail, but the suspense was excruciating. What was Tonio writing? Had he really had a breakthrough? Was he digging deep into his own emotions to bring life to his characters? Whenever she hinted that she'd like to read his new material, Tonio simply smiled and said, "You'll see it when it's done."

On the afternoon of the third day, he handed her a sheaf of papers. "Here it is, Ashley. You can read the hard copy, or you can read it on the computer. If you're like me, you like real paper and ink."

She accepted the manuscript with a look of wonder. Would she find the real Tonio in these pages? Had he truly made himself vulnerable for the sake of his characters? "I'll read it, but you can't watch me."

He stood up. "Fine. I'll go pester Mika for some more of those macadamia nut cookies."

She chuckled. "We finished those two days ago."

"Don't worry. There are more where those came from." He strolled out of the office, leaving her alone to read.

She went over to the sofa and sat down, curling her legs up under her. She wanted to read leisurely and savor every word. Her eyes scanned the first page.

•

Philip Holt had always been a man in control—of his life, his emotions, his future. He prided himself in mastering his environment, in orchestrating his days, in manipulating the people around him. He never second-guessed himself. He knew what he wanted, and he knew what it took to achieve

*his goals. If a human being could be invincible, he was
that man.*

*Until the day someone murdered the only woman he had
ever loved. . . .*

*The night of her funeral he went to her closet and buried
his face in her clothes. He breathed in the scent of her perfume.
He fell asleep hugging her pillow, imagining that he still held
her in his arms.*

*He discovered places within himself he had never known
existed—pockets of pain so intense he was convinced he was
having a heart attack. No one had ever told him a man
could die of a broken heart, but now he knew it was so.*

Ashley had to stop reading. Tears blurred her vision, and a
lump had formed in her throat, so painful she couldn't swallow.
She reached for a tissue, blew her nose, and blinked back the
tears. Now, at last, she knew how Tonio felt about Brianna. He
had finally confronted his grief. Now perhaps he could begin to
heal.

She continued reading. Every page was as vivid and compelling as the one before. It was as if a dam had broken in
Tonio's emotions. He was holding nothing back.

She didn't hear him return to the office until he set a plate
of cookies on the end table beside the sofa. She jumped,
startled, her hand flying to her chest. "Oh, my goodness. You
scared the life out of me!"

"I'm sorry. I didn't mean to disturb you."

"It's okay." She stood up and handed him the pages. "I was just
so caught up in the story." She looked up at him, tears running
down her cheeks. "It's incredible, Tonio. Your best writing ever.
You made my heart ache for Philip. I love it—every word."

Tonio beamed. "You mean it? You're not just saying what I
want to hear?"

"Would I do that?"

"Not for a minute."

"You've found your voice for this story," she went on, her excitement building. "It's no longer just a great suspense-adventure novel. It has the makings of a literary masterpiece. You'll win an award for this book, I'm sure of it."

He laughed. "You may be going a little overboard, but don't let me stop you."

"I'm serious. You've broken through that mental barrier. Your writing is so honest and vulnerable. So real."

"Thanks to you, my sweet little nag." Impulsively he gathered Ashley into his arms and swung her around, her feet flying in the air. "We did it, lady! You wouldn't let me get by with anything less."

When he set her down, her head was reeling and her knees weak. She realized he was still holding her in his arms, her head nestled against his chest. She could hear his heart pounding through his nylon shirt. After a moment, he tipped her chin up to his and kissed her soundly on the mouth. She returned the kiss, dazzled, the fragrance of his aftershave filling her nostrils. She had lived all her life for a moment like this. *Don't let me go, Tonio. Please. Never let me go!*

All too soon he released her and stumbled backward, bumping the desk. His face was flushed, his ebony hair cascading over his high forehead. "Wow! Talk about getting carried away." With the back of his hand he rubbed her lipstick from his mouth. "I'm sorry, Ashley. I didn't mean to do that. It was just such a wonderful relief to know you liked the writing."

"That's okay," she murmured, sinking down on the sofa. *Is that all it was to you? A kiss of gratitude? Don't you see that everything has changed between us?*

He sat down beside her and touched her face, tucking a strand of hair behind her ear. "I hope this won't change anything between us, Ashley." His clear blue eyes looked so earnest, so contrite. "I know I was out of line. It won't happen again. Please don't think less of me."

"I don't. I wouldn't." She blinked to keep back her tears.

"I can see you're upset. If it's any consolation, I'm as surprised as you are. I honestly didn't see that kiss coming." He raked his fingers through his tousled hair. "It was just one of those things. We've both been under a lot of pressure lately."

She nodded, afraid to speak lest she start to bawl. For a brilliant author, he sure could be a blockhead at times.

"Tell you what, Ashley." He gently stroked her cheek. "Let's quit work for today. What do you want to do? Go out to dinner? Or we could go over to the hotel in Keauhou and watch the manta rays. At night the locals watch them swim in the ocean under the bright lights beamed from the hotel."

She sniffed. "Why don't we save that for another time."

"Okay." His enthusiasm faded. "Do you just want to go back to your room and catch some shut-eye?"

She shook her head, still holding her tears in check.

"Then how about a swim in the pool? You do like to swim, don't you?"

She nodded, biting her lower lip.

"Great. Go change and meet me in the pool in ten minutes."

She nearly sprinted from the room. She couldn't wait to get back to her little cottage where she could release her pent-up emotions and let the dam break on her tears. She wept not only because the kiss had meant nothing to Tonio, but also because it had meant everything to her. She was falling in love with a man she could never have. How could this be happening to her so soon after her breakup with Ben? What was wrong with her that she could be in love with two men at once?

She vented to God as she washed her face. "Lord, I must be a terrible person to be so shallow, so fickle. No wonder You took Ben from me. You knew I didn't deserve him. Is this what it's like to be on the rebound? If so, I hate it. My emotions are all over the place. Do You want me to leave Hawaii and go home? But then I'll have to face Ben again. Lord, help me. I'm so confused."

She put her hair in a ponytail, then changed into her bathing suit.

By the time she got out to the pool, Tonio was already swimming. "Come on in," he called. "The water feels great."

She considered jumping off the diving board, then decided to slip in on the shallow end. The water was perfect—warm and refreshing, sparkling with diamonds of sunlight. Ignoring Tonio, she swam several laps. She would show him she wasn't fazed by his kiss. Finally, she stopped and treaded water, catching her breath.

Tonio swam over beside her. "You swim like a pro. I didn't know you could swim like that."

"You never asked. I was on the swim team in college."

"Care to race, say, ten laps?"

"Why not?"

He gave her a playful grin. "How about a movie on cable tonight? Winner picks the movie, loser makes popcorn."

"You're on!"

They swam to the deep end of the pool, Tonio gave the signal, and they both kicked off, swimming side by side. By the sixth lap she was ahead, but by the tenth, he had passed her by half a length. "I won," he declared, grabbing the edge of the pool. "You make the popcorn."

Catching up with him, she slammed her palm against the water, drenching him. He shook the water off and sent a shower back in her direction. She coughed as water went up her nose.

"This is war!" she rasped. She lunged forward, placed both hands on top of Tonio's head, and pushed him under the water. He came back up with a *whoosh*, grabbed her around the waist, and plunged back down, taking her with him. Holding her breath, she kicked and flailed until he released her. They both popped up out of the water, laughing and sputtering.

"You're a worthy opponent," he gasped.

"And don't—you—forget it." She choked out the words.

Tonio climbed out of the pool, then helped her out. They both collapsed on the grass, trying to catch their breath. He looked over at her. "I feel like a kid again."

She laughed. "I hope Mika and Harry weren't watching. They'll think we're crazy."

"So what? It was fun."

Her gaze lingered on his handsome, sun-bronzed face. "Yes, it was fun." She hadn't expected Tonio to be so playful and funny.

He scrambled to his feet and pulled her up. "We'll just have time to shower and change for dinner. I'll meet you in the dining room in half an hour."

"Make it an hour and I'll be there."

The evening turned out more pleasant than she had expected—a delicious dinner of salmon and sweet potatoes, then on to the great room for a movie of Tonio's choosing—a slapstick comedy—and brimming bowls of buttered popcorn. Tonio sat at one end of the sofa, she at the other. If any awkwardness remained over their afternoon kiss, neither of them admitted it.

When the movie was over Tonio walked her back to her cottage and playfully nudged her chin as he said good night. His mood was lighter than she had ever seen it. "Ashley, this has been one of the best days I can remember."

She couldn't quite muster up the same enthusiasm. "I'll never forget it either, Tonio."

"And you've forgiven me my faux pas?"

"There's nothing to forgive." *What I can't forgive is that the kiss meant nothing to you!*

"Good night then. Sleep tight. Don't let the bedbugs bite." He chuckled. "My mother used to say that to me every night. Not a very pleasant saying, now that I think of it."

She laughed in spite of herself. "My mom always had me recite the prayer asking God to take my soul if I died before I woke. You wouldn't believe how many times I lay awake worrying that I would die before morning."

"And then there are all the nursery rhymes with all the terrible hidden meanings that would scare kids out of their wits. But it's late, so I guess we'd better save them for another time."

She nodded. "Yes, another time. Good night, Tonio."

"Good night, Ashley. See you in the morning."

❧

Tonio may have achieved a breakthrough in his writing, but if Ashley assumed they had made a breakthrough in their relationship, she quickly realized how wrong she was. If anything, Tonio seemed more remote than ever. He spent the next two days writing while she edited his material. It was all work and no play. On Saturday he drove her to Waimea, where they had lunch and visited the Kamuela Museum. On Sunday they went to church, walked along the seawall, and had dinner at a quaint little bistro on the beach.

But for all their time together, their conversations seemed flat, superficial. It was a letdown after the excitement they had shared the previous week over his writing. Was he deliberately pushing her away? If so, why? Did he no longer need her now that his writing was on track? Was he so much a loner that another person in his life threatened his well-being? The questions kept piling up, but the answers remained elusive.

On Monday night Tonio left the house for another mysterious meeting. He was gone again on Tuesday night without a word of explanation. *He must be seeing someone,* Ashley told herself as she sat alone in her little cottage. *Otherwise, he would tell me where he's going. There would be no reason to keep it secret.*

And yet, Tonio didn't act like a man in love with some mystery woman. His mood was often solemn, even morose, as if he were mulling over weighty issues or struggling with some private torment.

I thought his bad mood stemmed from his writing problems, Ashley mused as she climbed into bed late Tuesday night. *But his writing is going well now. Why is Tonio still so glum?*

A thought came to her: *It's Brianna, his dead wife. She haunts this place. She haunts his mind. She won't leave him alone.*

"That's crazy," Ashley said aloud as she rolled over and fluffed her pillow. "I don't believe in ghosts. At least, not the kind that come back from the dead to haunt people. But the *memories* of Brianna—that's what could be haunting Tonio. What terrible thing happened in their relationship causing him such torment?"

Ashley fell asleep pondering those questions. Sometime in the night she awoke. Had she heard a gate creaking by the pool? She lay still, listening, her eyes scouring the darkness. A cool breeze wafted through the open windows. She climbed out of bed and looked out toward the pool.

A shadowed figure was walking past the gazebo, heading toward the woods. There was no question this time. It was Tonio!

Ashley pulled on a shirt, sandals, and cutoff jeans, grabbed a small flashlight, and slipped out of the cottage. She followed Tonio at a safe distance, padding cautiously through the thick underbrush. When she reached the clearing beside the cliff, she positioned herself near Brianna's memorial site, turned off her light and hid behind a sturdy palm.

Tonio was already there, standing, head bowed, facing the sculpted angel. He knelt down on one knee on the manicured grass, put his head in his hands, and remained like that for several minutes. Ashley heard him speak in a low, agonized voice, hardly more than a whisper. Was he speaking to Brianna? Praying? Ashley listened intently, but the only words she heard were, "Forgive me, Brianna. God forgive me!"

Forgive you for what? Ashley wondered. *What did you do that you so desperately need her forgiveness? And God's!*

A twig snapped under Ashley's sandal.

Tonio jumped to his feet and looked around. "Who's there?"

Ashley pressed her spine against the tree trunk and held her breath.

"Someone's there," Tonio insisted. "Who is it?"

Ashley's heart thundered in her chest—surely Tonio could hear it—but she remained stone-still. She watched through the thicket as Tonio stepped back and looked around. Her heart lurched. He was too close to the edge of the cliff. Another backward step and he would tumble a thousand feet to his death.

An anguished cry erupted from her throat. "Tonio, watch out!"

He turned abruptly, his foot sliding on the uneven slate, sending a spray of loose stones ricocheting into the black ocean below. He caught himself at the very edge and regained his footing.

"Ashley? Is that you?"

She stepped out of the shadows into the faint wedge of moonlight. "Yes."

He strode over and seized her wrist. "What are you doing here?"

She was trembling. "I know I shouldn't have come. I—I was afraid for you."

"You had no business coming here."

"I'm sorry."

Pushing his way through the brambles, Tonio led her through the murky woods back to the cottage, pulling her along as if she were a child requiring discipline. Ashley had never seen him so filled with rage.

When they reached her door, he released her and stared her down. "How dare you intrude on my privacy that way? I trusted you. You could have got us both killed out there tonight."

She was sobbing now. "I—I just wanted to help."

"Then don't sneak around scaring me out of my wits."

"I won't, Tonio. Never again."

"I'll hold you to that promise." As his wrath dissipated, his voice softened. "It's late. Go back to bed. Get some sleep." He rubbed the back of his neck, then turned on his heel and stalked off toward the main house.

ten

First thing the next morning Ashley started packing. She had had enough of Anthony Adler, with his mood swings and mysterious ways. And his behavior last night had proved he was more than finished with her.

"So let it be," she told herself stoically as she stuffed shirts and jeans into her suitcase. She had accomplished what she came here to do. Now it was time to move on.

She wasn't sure where she would go, but God would show her the way. Maybe she would look for a job at another publishing house. Ben would give her a good recommendation. Maybe Tonio would, too, once he got over his anger. She still shuddered when she thought of how furious he was with her on the cliff last night. How could she have been so foolish as to follow him like that? And so reckless? It must have been all those old Nancy Drew mysteries she had devoured as a teenager.

But this was real life, not some storybook whodunit. Instead of solving a mystery, she had angered and disappointed a man she deeply admired. There was only one thing to do—leave!

When she had finished packing she walked over to the main house for breakfast. She dreaded facing Tonio, but it had to be done. She wasn't going to be spineless and leave without a proper good-bye, although the thought had crossed her mind.

Tonio was already at the table, reading the paper and drinking his coffee. Seeing her, Mika flashed her usual smile. "Good morning, Miss Ashley."

"Good morning, Mika."

Ashley sat down across from Tonio. He put down his

newspaper and gave her a look she couldn't quite read—a smile on the surface but conflicted emotions underneath. "Hello, Ashley."

"Tonio." She couldn't summon any other words.

Mika poured her a cup of coffee, then brought out two plates of steaming buckwheat pancakes drenched in maple syrup.

"I can't eat all of these, Mika."

"Yes, you can, Miss Ashley. You need meat on your bones."

"I'm really not that hungry."

In a slightly brittle voice, Tonio urged, "Humor her, Ashley."

"I'll eat what I can, Tonio." He was making her feel like a scolded child. "Thank you for a wonderful breakfast, Mika."

"Don't thank me. Thank the good Lord."

"I was just about to," said Tonio. He bowed his head and murmured a prayer. Ashley could tell his heart wasn't quite in it. Then he attacked his stack of hotcakes without a glance her way.

She took a few bites then set down her fork. She wasn't hungry. No use pretending she was. She cleared her throat. *Might as well get this over with now.* "Tonio, I—I have something to tell you."

He stopped sipping his coffee. "What is it?"

Her heart hammered. "I'll be leaving today."

"Leaving?" His cup clattered on its saucer. He stared at her as if he hadn't heard her clearly. "Going where?"

"Back to New York." Her words tumbled out in a rush. "I called the airlines. I might be able to get a standby flight out today. If not, I'll get a hotel room until a flight is available."

He shoved his plate away. She winced at the shock and outrage on his face. It wasn't supposed to go like this. She had expected him to be glad she was going.

"Why on earth are you leaving? Our work isn't done. You haven't given me any notice."

Her lower lip trembled. Why was he making this so hard for her? Why couldn't he just let her go in peace? "Tonio, you know why I'm going."

"Because of last night?"

She lowered her gaze. "Yes. You made it clear I'm no longer welcome here."

"I did no such thing." He slammed his fist on the table, shaking the china dishes. "Okay, so I got mad. I never dreamed you'd follow me out there to the cliff. I didn't even know you knew about that spot."

"I was wrong to follow you. I'm sorry."

He sat back and drew in a deep breath. "Fine. I accept your apology. Now let's just forget the whole thing."

"I can't."

"What do you mean, you can't?"

"I mean, I can't live like this, never knowing whether you're going to be in a good mood or a bad one. I just went through a painful breakup with Ben. I need some peace and stability in my life. I thought I could find it here, but I was wrong."

Tonio's expression softened. "No, Ashley, you weren't wrong. This is exactly where you should be. I was upset last night, but I shouldn't have taken it out on you."

"It's not just last night," she said, struggling for words. "I don't understand you—your mood swings, your aloofness. I never know whether you're going to be friendly or distant. You don't let anyone get close to you."

His brow furrowed. "I didn't realize I had made life so miserable for you."

"You haven't. I've loved working for you. It's just—"

"Just what?"

"I just think it's time for me to go."

"Think it over, and in a few days, if you still feel the same way. . ."

"I'm already packed," she mumbled, fighting back tears.

His voice thickened. "Then go unpack. You're not getting away that easily. You can't just walk out on me because I lost my temper."

"I think it would be best." She sounded so lame. She had rehearsed an entire speech in her mind, but it was gone now.

Tonio reached across the table for her hand. "Finish breakfast. Then we'll talk, okay?"

She withdrew her hand and picked without interest at her food.

When they had finished eating, he said, "Listen, Ashley, I'll make a deal with you. Promise you'll stay until I've finished writing my novel. Then if you still want to leave, I won't say a word."

She lifted her chin decisively. "Just the first draft."

"Final draft. Please."

"First draft. That's all I can promise for now."

Tonio's blue eyes blazed. "Then I guess there's nothing more to say." He pushed back his chair, stood up, crumpled his napkin, and tossed it on his plate. "Mika, I'm going to run some errands in town. Don't wait on me for lunch."

"Yes, Mr. Adler. You have a good day, sir."

He glanced down at Ashley. "I don't suppose you want to go with me."

"No, thank you. I—I have some research to do."

"And some unpacking?"

"That, too."

Even after Tonio strode out the door, a chill remained in the air. As Mika cleared the table, Ashley finished her coffee and nursed her hurt feelings. Would she ever feel close to Tonio again, or would there always be this feeling of unease between them?

"Miss Ashley, don't pay Mr. Adler no mind," said Mika as she refilled her coffee cup. "He don't mean to be so gruff. He's a broken man. You're the first to make him smile again."

Ashley nodded. "I know he's still mourning his wife's death. I wish I knew how to help him."

"He don't let nobody help him." Mika carried the sugar bowl and salt and pepper shakers to the kitchen.

"How did she die?" asked Ashley. It was the question she had never dared ask Tonio.

Mika returned to the table for the cups and saucers. "You talking about Mrs. Adler?"

"Yes. Did she have an illness? Cancer?"

Mika stopped and gave Ashley a curious glance. For a moment, Ashley thought Mika wasn't going to answer. Finally she solemnly replied, "Mrs. Adler was never sick a day in her life. She died in a car crash."

Ashley looked up, startled. "Oh? I hadn't realized it was an accident. I just assumed. . ." She let her voice trail off.

"Mr. Adler never forgave himself," said Mika in a hushed voice. "He never mentions her name."

"Was she alone, Mika? Alone in the car?"

"No. Mr. Adler was with her. He lived. She died."

"Where did it happen?"

"Not far away. A mile maybe. On the winding road near here."

"You mean the road that winds along the cliffs to this house?"

Mika nodded. "The car went over the cliff into the water. Mrs. Adler drowned."

An icy shiver shot through Ashley as she pictured Tonio standing at the edge of the precipice, near Brianna's memorial, staring down into the turbulent sea below. *No wonder he's so obsessed with the ocean surging a thousand feet below him. It claimed the love of his life!*

Ashley got up from the table. "Thanks for everything, Mika. I'm going to the office to do some research."

"Miss Ashley?"

"Yes, Mika?"

"Please don't leave Mr. Adler. He needs you. Don't go."

"I won't, Mika. At least, not right away."

On her way to the office, Ashley paused by Brianna's portrait. The face and eyes were more haunting now than ever, bespeaking a tragedy Ashley couldn't even imagine. What secrets were locked behind the unseeing eyes of that painting? Why had Tonio never mentioned how his wife died? What else was he hiding behind his handsome, mysterious, ironclad veneer?

It's time to do some sleuthing of my own. I've got to know more. I can't let this go until I know exactly what happened.

Ashley opened her laptop on Tonio's desk, logged on to the Internet, and began browsing several search engines. *I don't know why I never thought of this before. There should be dozens of articles about Tonio online. What was the date of death on Brianna's memorial angel? September something. Yes, that's it—September 17, 2003.*

Ashley found countless articles on Tonio and his books, but they covered little of his personal life. Clearly he was a private man who knew how to keep himself out of the limelight. Ashley tried another tactic. She typed in "Brianna Adler, wife of Anthony Adler," and several tabloid articles appeared. The headline of one screamed out at Ashley: FAMED AUTHOR'S WIFE DIES IN CAR CRASH.

Ashley quickly scanned the article. The details were horrifying. The couple was on their way home from a party given to celebrate the release of a movie based on one of Tonio's books. The car swerved off a mountain cliff near their home and plunged into the ocean. Tonio was able to get out of the car and swim free. By the time he returned to rescue his wife, she had perished.

Ashley's gaze lingered on the last paragraph.

Authorities refuse comment until they have finished investigating the accident. Questions remain as to who was driving the vehicle. Mr. Adler, who, according to test results, had been drinking heavily, could be held on a manslaughter charge if it is proved he was behind the wheel. Some who witnessed the couple arguing heatedly at the party speculate that the crash may not have been an accident after all.

Ashley shuddered, her thoughts reeling. Everything she had ever known about Anthony Adler was suddenly suspect. Who was this man she had imagined she loved? A drunkard? She had never seen him drink a drop of alcohol. A murderer? Inconceivable! And yet the words blazed in black and white on her computer screen. A drunken Anthony Adler had apparently caused his wife's death!

Ashley desperately scanned other articles, praying they would exonerate him. But they all suggested the same thing— Tonio was likely driving the fated vehicle when it made its death-plunge into the churning Pacific. But because it couldn't be proved, charges were never filed.

Ashley sat back, stunned. She couldn't take it all in, couldn't wrap her mind around the malevolent portrait the articles painted. How had she not seen this dark side of him? Or had she been too blinded by love to see the truth? Was Tonio really the monster the tabloids presented?

Ashley closed her laptop with trembling fingers. *I've got to get out of here. I can't stay another night. I can't look Tonio in the eyes again. He'll see the horror in my face. He'll know I know what he did.*

She stood up. *What to do now? I'm already packed. I'll leave before Tonio gets home. I'll phone for a taxi. Yes, that's it, a taxi.*

She reached for the phone, but it rang before she could dial. She jumped, startled, then answered with a tentative, "Hello."

The voice that replied was both foreign and familiar. "Ashley? Is that you? This is Ben."

Her mind was moving in slow motion. "Ben?"

"Yes, I'm calling for Tonio. Is he there?"

"No. He—he went into town. He'll be back after lunch."

"Okay, fine. Will you give him a message for me?"

She sat back down and reached for a pad of paper. "Yes, Ben, what is it?"

"Tell him I loved the last chapters. They're the best he's ever done."

"I'll tell him." Her mind was spinning away somewhere in space. She couldn't focus on Ben's words. When he said, "I'll see you tomorrow," she was sure she had misunderstood.

"Did you hear me, Ashley?"

"No, I'm sorry, Ben. It sounded like you said you would see me."

"Yes. Tomorrow. I'm flying to Kona in the morning."

"You're coming here? Why?"

"I have some business to discuss with Tonio, and I think it's time we conferred in person about his book. I like the direction he's taking, but I have some ideas to make it stronger." He paused for a long moment, then said in a voice she couldn't quite read, "And since I have some vacation time coming, I thought I'd combine business and pleasure. I look forward to seeing you again, Ashley."

She tried to reply, but panic tightened in her throat.

"Ashley? Are you still there?"

"Yes," she managed. "I'm here. But not for long. I'm leaving Kona. Today."

"Leaving? Why?"

"Please, Ben, don't ask. It's too complicated to explain."

"You can't leave yet," he admonished. "You've become vital to this project. Stay at least through my visit. It'll be a few days at most. Then we can fly home together."

She was too emotionally spent to argue. "All right. I'll stay. Do you want Tonio to pick you up at the airport?"

"No need. I'll take a taxi. I should be there late tomorrow afternoon."

After hanging up the phone, Ashley left a note for Tonio, then went to the kitchen where Mika was polishing the silver. Ashley told her to expect an extra houseguest, then announced that she had a headache and was going back to the cottage to rest. "Tell Tonio I'm skipping dinner. I'm not feeling well."

"I'll tell him, Miss Ashley. Later I'll bring you some tea and toast. You get some rest now. You look white as a ghost."

Ashley smiled grimly. "I've definitely had better days, Mika."

As she tramped back to the cottage, Ashley mused that she would be spending the next few days with two men she loved—one had broken her heart, and the other was living a lie. How on earth was she going to keep her sanity intact?

eleven

I'll be seeing Ben again. . .seeing Ben again. Ashley woke the next morning with that refrain playing in her mind. It had been over three months since their fateful wedding day. Three months since their painful breakup on the beach. *How will I feel, seeing him again? How will he feel about me?*

She didn't want to admit that she was looking forward to seeing her ex-fiancé. Since their breakup, she had struggled to shut the door on her memories of Ben. She had locked her grief away in a little room in her heart—a spot she refused to visit these days lest the pain rush back and overwhelm her. But now she would have to confront those feelings. The idea terrified and tantalized her at the same time. *What's wrong with you, girl?* she chided herself as she scoured her closet for her most flattering outfit. *Get yourself together. Ben's out of your life for good. Why are you trying to impress him?*

"I don't know," she said aloud. "I just am. So there!"

She tried on a tropical-print slip dress and decided it was too dressy. She pulled on a cotton jersey shirt and white jeans and decided they were too casual. She finally settled on a blue tie-shoulder top and white cotton gauze skirt. Blue was Ben's favorite color.

Ashley skipped breakfast so she wouldn't have to face Tonio. By the time she arrived at the main house, he was already busy preparing for Ben's arrival. She cleared Tonio's desktop and organized the latest draft of his novel, hoping he wouldn't notice she was avoiding him. As much as she wanted him to explain his part in his wife's death, she knew she couldn't handle a confrontation with Tonio when she was about to see Ben again.

Late that afternoon she found herself watching out the window for Ben's taxi. Tonio noticed and said, "If his plane was delayed it could be another hour yet."

"I wasn't watching for him," she said quickly, as if she needed to explain herself.

"He'll probably call on his cell when he lands."

She played with the tie on her shoulder strap. "Right. I hadn't thought of that."

Tonio gave her a look she couldn't quite decipher—concern, irritation, jealousy? "Is this going to be hard on you, having him here?"

She looked away. "No, why should it?"

"You were about to marry the guy—until he made the biggest blunder of his life and walked away."

"That's over. In the past. I'll be fine. It's certainly not your problem."

His expression hardened. "You're right. It's not my problem. But we have a lot of work to do, and the last thing I need is a distracted assistant."

She bristled. "Have I ever allowed my personal life to interfere with my work?"

He backed down, his blue eyes warming with unmistakable affection. "I apologize, Ashley. You've done an extraordinary job. I don't know what I would have done without you."

"Thank you, Tonio." Her indignation evaporated, leaving her feeling suddenly vulnerable to his charms. She looked back out the window. "I think I see him. A taxi—coming up the drive."

A minute later she was opening the door to Ben, greeting him as if it were the most natural thing in the world. In his gray pinstripe suit he looked taller than she remembered. His short blond hair was stylishly tousled and his hazel eyes twinkled behind his trendy wire-rim glasses.

"Ashley, you look beautiful!" He embraced her with greater vigor than she anticipated. For an instant she felt as if she had never left his arms. But almost as quickly, the pain over their broken romance flooded back. "You look great, too, Ben," she said, gently extricating herself from his grasp.

Stepping between them, Tonio gripped Ben's hand and gave him a comradely slap on the back. "Welcome, ol' man. Great to see you again. How was your flight?"

Ben chuckled. "I suppose any flight you walk away from is a good one. But I'm not crazy about all those long hours over the ocean."

"We're a long way from the mainland. Well, I hope you're hungry. Mika is putting on a feast tonight."

"Are you kidding? After all those cold meals at the local delicatessen, I'm always ready for Mika's home cooking."

Tonio stepped out on the porch and gathered up Ben's suitcase, laptop, and briefcase. "I've got your luggage. Let's get you settled in your room."

Ben reached for the suitcase. "Thanks, Tonio. I'll take it."

"No trouble, Ben. I've got it. I'll take it upstairs. Then you can get yourself out of that monkey suit and into some Hawaiian duds. One thing we like around here is comfort. Right, Ashley?"

"Right. If you didn't bring your aloha shirt, Tonio has plenty."

"A whole closet full, if I remember right," said Ben.

"Anything to keep from being strangled by a dress shirt and tie," said Tonio.

As the two men strode on down the hall, laughing and making small talk, Ashley sensed a friendly, unspoken rivalry between them. She couldn't help wondering: Was it because of her?

Dinner that evening was bizarre, surreal. Ashley felt a little like Alice in Wonderland at the Mad Hatter's tea party. Sitting at the same table with the two men she cared so much about, she felt somehow on trial, her every word and action scrutinized. Most curious of all, she had the distinct impression that both men were vying for her attention like capricious schoolboys. She had never heard them tell so many jokes or share so many stories, each seemingly trying to outdo the other.

"Ben, do you remember that offbeat awards show?" said Tonio. "I can't even remember the name of it now—where they gave me that gold-plated statuette that must have weighed fifty pounds?"

Ben nodded. "And after the show we went to that little diner off Fifth Avenue and you left the award sitting in the booth."

"Right. And the waitress—"

"Thought it was a tip."

Tonio chuckled. "She was downright indignant when I asked for it back. Can you believe that, Ashley?"

She looked up from her plate. "I'm sorry. My mind wandered. What did you say?"

"Never mind," said Tonio with a wry smile. "You had to be there."

Ben leaned over and patted her hand. "Are you feeling all right, Ashley? You're so quiet tonight. And you look a little pale."

She set her napkin on the table. "The truth is, I have a headache. Would you two mind if I excused myself and went back to the cottage?"

Tonio pushed his chair back. "We should all make an early evening of it. Ben, you're still on New York time. It's six hours later there."

"Don't remind me."

"Then let's all call it a night," said Tonio. "We'll have an early breakfast and a full schedule tomorrow."

Ashley jumped up, almost toppling her chair. "Good night, then, Ben, Tonio. I'll see you both in the morning." Before either of them could reply, she turned on her heel and hurried from the room. Perhaps she was foolish to run off like that, but how could she go on pretending everything was normal, when one man had rejected her and the other was hiding a deadly secret?

⁊⧫

The next day Ashley focused on the work at hand with such diligence that she managed to keep her mind off her personal life. Both Tonio and Ben congratulated her on her sharp editorial skills and extraordinary intuition.

"Ashley, you're a gem," said Tonio approvingly. "You have an innate sense about these characters. It's as if you had created them yourself."

Ben agreed. "I tell you, Tonio, she has a knack for pin-pointing exactly what's wrong with a plot line or reworking a character who's false or inconsistent. She's transformed every book she's edited. Do you see why I hated to lose her?"

An uneasy silence settled over them. Ashley wanted to cry out, *If you hated to lose me, Ben, why did you break up with me?*

Ben cleared his throat. "Like I said, Ashley was a hard assistant to lose. Her replacement doesn't have half the talent she has."

"And now you know why I don't want to let her go," said Tonio. "She's challenged me in ways I never expected—creatively, I mean."

"Hello already. You don't have to talk about me in the third person," said Ashley dryly. "I'm still here in the room."

They both laughed, prompting a reluctant chuckle from her.

Over the next few days they worked exhaustively on Tonio's novel, debating plot points, polishing scenes, and tightening the writing. Ashley could see that Ben was more than pleased with the results.

"Well, our marathon editing session has proved amazingly fruitful." He patted the stack of manuscript pages on the desk. "Tonio, this book is your best by far. The way you've explored the emotional lives of your characters and revealed their vulnerabilities is superb. I think it's time we discuss a sequel, maybe several sequels."

Tonio raked his fingers through his tousled hair. "Let's get this one into galleys first, Ben."

"I know you'll need some breathing room. But I'm ready to talk contracts with your agent. I think you'll find the terms impressive. More to the point, presales are looking good, so Haricott is ready to put some solid backing behind this novel. Talk shows, book tours, print and TV ads, reviews in the top newspapers and magazines."

Tonio rubbed his jaw thoughtfully. "Sounds good."

"That's only the half of it," said Ben. "I don't know if your agent has notified you yet, but based on the synopsis he distributed to several major Hollywood producers, at least three are ready to bid on the movie rights. Think of it, Tonio. Another motion picture deal."

Tonio's countenance darkened. "I don't know, Ben. I'm not sure I can handle a production company messing with my work again. You know how bad it was last time."

"You can't judge everything by that experience, Tonio. You need this. Your career needs it."

"Why don't we take a break? I'm famished," said Ashley, sensing Tonio's unease. "Then we can talk again after dinner."

"Good idea," said Ben, his eyes brightening. "Let's celebrate. Tonio, you pick your favorite restaurant in Kona, and we'll make an evening of it. My treat. No work, all play."

"Now that's a deal I can't refuse," said Ashley, looking to Tonio for his response.

He nodded. "Guess I'd better make it unanimous."

"If you know what's good for you," said Ben with a grin.

"Is this party formal or come as you are?" asked Ashley.

"Your call," said Tonio. "Do you want to walk on the beach with the sand between your toes or strut around in your three-inch heels and dressiest dress?"

Usually Ashley would have opted for the beach, but tonight she heard herself reply, "Let's go dressy."

"Then I know just the place," said Tonio. "We'll drive up the coast to Waikoloa, to one of the largest, fanciest oceanfront resorts on the Big Island. Sixty acres of paradise. They have a variety of restaurants, but my favorite has Italian cuisine."

"Naturally, you'd love it," said Ashley. "You're Italian."

"You'll love it, too. It's a fantastic place."

Ashley sprang to her feet. "Then what are we waiting for?"

An hour later they met in Tonio's marble entryway and gazed at one another with approving smiles.

"Hey, we clean up pretty good," said Ben. He was wearing a black suit with a lavender shirt and paisley tie.

Tonio had on black trousers, a white dinner jacket, and black bow tie. "But when it comes to looking fine," he noted, "Ashley wins, hands down."

"No question about it," said Ben. "You look gorgeous, Ashley."

"Thank you, gentlemen." She did a spontaneous little pirouette in her powder blue empire-waist gown and stiletto heels.

"So let's get this show on the road," said Tonio, stepping in front of Ben to escort Ashley out the door. "We have reservations for eight o'clock sharp."

From the moment they stepped into the dazzling resort at Waikoloa, Ashley knew the evening was going to be magical. To her surprise, her earlier uneasiness around Tonio and Ben was gone. She felt happy, relaxed, simply enjoying the company of two men she cared about and who obviously cared about her. Nothing heavy or complicated. Just three good friends enjoying one another's company.

They walked through the enormous lobby with its rows of huge potted palms and a centerpiece of dolphin sculptures. They watched bullet-shaped Swiss trams whiz by and stood on a bridge over a winding waterway watching canal boats take guests from one end of the resort to the other. They scaled the grand staircase and gazed down at the sprawling lagoon with its crystal pools, sparkling waterfalls, and tropical gardens. Beyond the white sand beach, a blue-velvet ocean cut a swath across an azure, star-studded sky.

"I'm on top of the world!" Ashley exclaimed, spreading her arms.

And as she descended the wide marble stairs with her handsome escorts, one on each arm, she felt like Cinderella at the ball. *I don't care if I go back to rags and cinders tomorrow; I'm going to have the time of my life tonight!*

They were seated at a linen-draped table on the lanai along the waterway; a bouquet of tropical flowers graced the table; a guitarist strummed romantic melodies nearby.

"This place is amazing," said Ashley as the waiter placed her linen napkin on her lap. "A little taste of heaven on earth."

"Wait 'til you taste the food," said Tonio, opening his menu.

Ashley ordered the fried calamari with saffron pepper sauce; Ben selected the veal scallopini with sautéed mushrooms in asparagus cream sauce; and Tonio decided on the cannelloni stuffed with veal, spinach, and ricotta cheese.

After a leisurely dinner with spumoni ice cream for dessert, they browsed the quaint shops. But the guys seemed bored, so she suggested a walk along the lagoon. Before leaving the shop, Tonio bought her a shell necklace and Ben, not wanting to be outdone, bought her a stuffed dolphin. Hugging her treasures to her chest, Ashley thanked them both. "You two are making me feel like a pampered child."

"Just a small token of our appreciation," said Tonio with a wink.

"If I'd known a stuffed dolphin would make you happy, I'd have bought you one a long time ago," said Ben.

She grinned impishly. "No, it'll take more than that."

Tonio nudged Ben. "Guess she put you in your place. Last of the big-time spenders."

"You think you scored points with your little string of seashells?" countered Ben. "They're a dime a dozen."

Ashley broke in. "Stop it, you guys. I love my gifts. They'll always remind me of tonight and your good company."

"See, Tonio?" said Ben. "She likes our company."

"What choice does she have? She's stuck with us for the evening."

She wove her arms through theirs. "There's nowhere I'd rather be than right here with the two of you. We've just finished a huge project—a literary masterpiece, no less—so we have every right to celebrate."

"Well put," said Ben.

They walked in step, arms linked. "If we keep this up, they'll call us the Three Musketeers," said Tonio.

Ben chuckled. "Did you say, Mouseketeers?"

"You've been watching too much kiddie TV," said Tonio.

"You guys are spoiling the mood," said Ashley. "Let's just walk around quietly and enjoy the scenery."

"You hear that, Tonio?" said Ben. "You're spoiling the mood."

"Not me. It's you."

"It's both of you," said Ashley. "No one would guess one of you is a temperamental author and the other a stuffy editor."

"Stuffy, am I?" Ben shot back.

"I don't have a temperamental bone in my body," declared Tonio.

"Okay, okay. You're both paragons of virtue. Now can we just go watch the dolphins?"

For the next hour they strolled around the lagoon, watching the dolphins and listening to the rhythmic, rushing roar of the waves. Dozens of towering palm trees were silhouetted against the sky, and tiki torches lighted the pathway. Wide hammocks were strung between trees on the grassy area by the beach with white sand pits beneath them.

"Look! I love these!" Ashley sat down tentatively on one of the hammocks and kicked off her shoes. She put her feet up and lay back. "Okay, you guys, I've found my perfect spot."

Tonio gave the hammock a push. It rocked gently from side to side. "Looks good to me. What do you think, Ben?"

"Looks perfect. Let's try it."

Tonio climbed in on one side and Ben on the other.

"What are you guys doing?" cried Ashley. "Get your own hammock."

"We like this one," said Ben. They both lay back, sandwiching Ashley in the middle. They rocked the hammock, making it sway.

"This is crazy," Ashley protested. "We're like sardines. I can't breathe."

Tonio shifted his weight, making the hammock swing harder, faster. Ashley started to laugh. She couldn't stop, even though her stomach ached and her eyes teared. The threesome rollicked with laughter until the hammock shuddered and rolled. Suddenly it tipped and the three of them toppled out, one after another, sprawling in the sand like rag dolls in formal wear. Tonio and Ben scrambled to their feet and helped her up. She straightened her gown, retrieved her shoes, and gathered up her shell necklace and stuffed dolphin. Tonio brushed sand from her chin and smoothed back her mussed hair.

"I must look like I got in a fight with a hammock, and the hammock won," she said, still on the verge of laughter. "Is my mascara running?"

Tonio rubbed his thumb under her eyes. "You could look like a raccoon, and you'd still be beautiful."

"Not exactly Shakespeare," said Ben, "but a good try, Tonio."

"Think you can do better, Ben? Let's hear your feeble attempts at poetry."

"Come on, you guys," said Ashley. "It's been a wonderful night. But isn't it time to go home?"

The three of them headed back to the car, making silly jokes and laughing all the way, as if they had imbibed more than sparkling cider, the two men behaving more like suitors than colleagues. Ashley sensed there would never be another night like this in her life. Someday, when she was a little old lady, she would still recall with yearning and delight this marvelous evening she had shared with two such extraordinary men.

twelve

I hope the two of you don't mind keeping each other company tonight," Tonio told Ashley and Ben at lunch the next day. "I have an appointment in town tonight. A dinner meeting. I may be late."

Ashley's heart sank at the idea of Tonio going off to another of his mysterious meetings. "Do you have to go tonight?" she asked. "This is Ben's last night here."

"I'm sorry, Ashley. It can't be helped."

"Don't sweat it, Tonio," said Ben with a sidelong glance at Ashley. "We'll get by just fine. We could watch a movie, take a swim, or even drive into town. What do you say, Ashley?"

She shrugged, swallowing her disappointment. "Since you're leaving tomorrow, Ben, it should be your decision."

"All right, maybe we'll relax on the lanai and listen to the ocean. That's something I can't do this time of the year in New York."

Tonio gave Ben a squint-eyed glance, as if to say, *Don't get too cozy.* Or was Ashley just reading into Tonio's expression what she wanted to see?

That evening, with Tonio gone, dinner felt almost like a date. She and Ben sat across from each other while Mika served them a delectable meal of barbecued chicken, fried potatoes, green beans, and fresh pineapple. Ashley had mixed feelings about being alone with Ben. She couldn't help remembering the many times they had dined together at some of New York's poshest restaurants. Ben had always showered her with the best—long-stemmed red roses, expensive perfume, rare chocolate delicacies, the most popular concerts and plays in town. But mingled with the happy memories were the tears she had shed and the humiliation she had felt when he left her at the altar.

After dinner, Ben suggested they take a swim.

She thought a minute then said, "I'd rather just relax by the pool."

He smiled affably. "We can do that, too. I'll put on some music and we can sit on the lanai and catch up on our lives. Maybe swap stories about what's happened over the past few months."

You mean, you want to know what I've been doing since you dumped me? She dismissed her silent retort. "You know what I've been doing. Working for Tonio."

They walked out to the lanai and sat down on adjoining lounge chairs near the pool. "I'm talking about your personal life, Ashley."

She stretched out her legs, smoothed her sundress, and rested her head against the back of the chair. "There hasn't been much of a personal life, Ben."

"I know Tonio has kept you busy."

"Yes, he has. But I've enjoyed working on his book."

"It's a great read. He owes you a debt of gratitude. He's achieved an emotional resonance I haven't seen in his earlier work."

"It wasn't all me. He finally allowed himself to tap into his buried feelings about his wife's death."

"That wouldn't have happened without you, Ashley."

"I like to think that's true." She looked over at Ben. "Why didn't you tell me his wife died in a car crash?"

"I guess the subject never came up."

"I never thought to ask. I assumed it was an illness or something."

"From the beginning Tonio made it clear he didn't want to discuss his wife's death, so we at Haricott respected his wishes."

Ashley ran her fingers over the arm of her chair. "Did you know he was in the car? He had been drinking. The authorities even considered pressing manslaughter charges against him."

"He wasn't driving," said Ben.

"How do you know?"

"He told me."

She gazed out at the bright orange sun hovering over the glistening sea. "And you believed him?"

"I had no reason not to. What did he tell you?"

"Nothing. I read it on the Internet. He doesn't know I know."

"Why not?"

She shrugged. "He's such a private man. I didn't know how to bring it up. And I didn't want him to feel obligated to tell me when he's tried so hard to forget."

"He is a private man, that's for sure," agreed Ben. "Where do you suppose he is tonight?"

"I don't know. He goes out like this a couple of nights a week. I think maybe he's seeing someone."

"Dating?"

Ashley tried to sound nonchalant. "Is that so hard to believe?"

After a long pause, Ben said, "Frankly, I think he has quite a crush on you."

Ashley laughed. "Ben, you're imagining things. He's still madly in love with his wife. If he is seeing someone, it's because he's trying to forget Brianna."

"You may be right."

"The truth is," she said, her voice tremulous, "I was so disturbed about Tonio's past and his secretive behavior, I was ready to leave here. I would have, too, but then you called to say you were coming to Kona."

"Yes, I remember you mentioned leaving. What do you mean by Tonio's secretive behavior?"

She examined the cuticle of one polished nail, debating whether to broach the subject with Ben.

"Ashley?" he prompted.

Before she knew it, the words came tumbling out. "Oh,

Ben, it's so frightening—Tonio's so tormented with guilt. It's a terrible thing to live with—the idea that he killed the love of his life."

"What are you saying, Ashley?"

"I've followed him, Ben." She brushed sudden tears from her cheeks. "Tonio goes to his wife's grave on the cliff near here. Sometimes he just stands and stares out at the ocean, as if in a trance. One night I was afraid he was going to. . ." She couldn't say the word.

Ben's eyebrows shot up. "Jump?"

"I don't think he would have. But for a moment I was petrified. And when he realized I was watching, he became enraged. I had never seen him like that."

Ben put his hand on hers. "Maybe it is time for you to go home."

"I can't." She was trembling. "I'm afraid for him, Ben. I'm afraid he's going to get so caught up in his grief he'll throw himself over the cliff. He's so closed up; he doesn't want anyone to know who he really is inside. I've learned the only way anyone can know him is through his writing, and even then it's through a veil of fiction."

"Ashley, listen to me," said Ben. "You can't rush in and save him from himself. His problems are too complicated for you to solve."

"I know." She leaned her head back and closed her eyes. "I know there's nothing I can do for Tonio, except help him with his writing. I've got to stay until his book is done."

"You can finish the editing in New York. We can always find a place for you again at Haricott."

She wanted to ask, *What am I going home to? A broken romance? Working beside the man who hurt me so deeply?*

He seemed to read her mind, for he said, "I know I made a mess of things. And if you don't want to work with me, I'm sure we can make other arrangements."

She withdrew her hand. "I don't know what I want, Ben.

I don't know what God wants for me. At first I thought He wanted me to marry you. Then I thought He wanted me to be here in Kona to help Tonio. I've prayed and prayed about it, but I have no idea what I'm supposed to do."

Gently Ben turned her face toward his. "Listen, Ashley. Maybe I have some answers for you."

The intensity in his eyes made her uneasy. "What answers, Ben?"

His gaze was riveting, his hazel eyes crinkling at the corners the way she had once adored. "I want you back, Ashley. I was crazy to let you go." For an instant he was the old Ben, the one who had courted her and won her heart. But just as quickly she recalled the day on the beach he betrayed her trust.

"Ashley, did you hear me? I still love you."

No, no! This wasn't what she wanted to hear now. She jumped up and walked over to the edge of the pool. A breeze was gusting in from the ocean. She hugged herself, shivering.

Ben came up behind her and placed his hands on her shoulders. "Ashley, I didn't come to Hawaii just to work on Tonio's manuscript. Or even for a vacation. You must have known. I came here to see you, to find out if there's still a chance for the two of us."

She shook her head, stunned. "Ben, are you serious?"

He turned her around to face him. The lowering sun cast a burnished glow on his handsome features. "When I got back to New York, I couldn't believe how empty my life felt without you. Everywhere I went I kept expecting to see you. I kept going to church, because it made me feel close to you. And finally it started getting through to me. What I loved about you was your faith, your trust in God, and the way His love shone through you. I wanted that kind of life for myself."

Tears of frustration welled in her eyes. "You should have realized that before our wedding day, Ben, before you humiliated me in front of the whole world."

He brushed a tear from her cheek. "I know. It took losing

you for me to realize what I really wanted." He rubbed her arm, his sturdy hand warm and soothing on her cold skin. "I've committed my life to Christ, Ashley," he said softly, "not just for you, but for myself. I'm not pretending anymore. I'm not just playing church."

"Stop it, Ben! You're just telling me what you think I want to hear."

"I'm not, Ashley, I promise you. Because no matter what you decide to do, I'm building a relationship with God. At church, I'm involved in the weekly Bible study and Men's Fellowship. Spiritually, I'm still a newborn. I know I've got so much to learn, but I'm reading the Bible and praying. And now I'm beginning to understand what you were trying to tell me all along."

Ashley stared at him, her mind whirling.

"You believe me, don't you, Ashley?"

She pushed his hand away, anger turning sour in her throat. "How can you use my faith to twist the dagger deeper? This is just a game you're playing. You think by saying all the right things I'll forget what happened and rush back into your arms."

"No, sweetheart, I don't think that. I won't blame you if you want nothing to do with me. But I had to let you know I've changed."

She inhaled deeply, steadying her breath. "If you've truly accepted Christ into your life, I'm happy for you. I've prayed that God would speak to your heart and bring you to faith in Him. But it doesn't change anything between us. It's over, Ben. It was over when you walked away from me on our wedding day."

He removed his glasses and lowered his gaze; a muscle twitched beside his mouth. "It's Tonio, isn't it?"

"Don't, Ben."

"It's true." He rubbed the bridge of his nose and replaced his glasses. "I can feel the connection between you two. I see it even if you don't admit it. You're in love with him."

thirteen

Early the next morning Ashley got up, showered, and dressed, all the while thinking of the two men in her life. A few months ago she had loved Ben and was ready to spend her life with him, but now her heart was drawn to Tonio. But the most important question was: What did God want for her now?

Lost in thought, she went to her kitchenette, made coffee, and took it out to the little table on her lanai. She sat watching the sky as vibrant colors of morning washed over the rocky shoals—soft lavenders, pinks, and powder blues. Birds twittered and rustled the leaves of the plumeria trees. A gentle breeze wafted through distant date palms like a whisper from God.

"Lord, I need to hear Your voice," she murmured. "My life seems to be going in so many directions at once. What do You want me to do? Where do You want me to go? And who do You want me to be with?"

Maybe she was asking the wrong questions. Maybe God didn't want her with Tonio or Ben. Maybe He wanted her to be alone. At least for now. Or maybe His plan for her life was something she hadn't even dreamed of yet. "Father, it's so hard not knowing what I'm supposed to do. Sometimes I feel cut adrift, aimless, going nowhere. Help me to do what pleases You. Right now I have no idea what that is."

She sipped her coffee, her thoughts swinging back and forth between Ben and Tonio. When she thought of Ben, she thought of all they had meant to each other. She remembered their dates in New York, their days of working together at the publishing house. Their minds were always in sync; they looked at things the same way, always knowing what to expect from the other. There was a lovely security in being with someone she knew so well.

But you didn't know him as well as you thought. He gave no advance warning when he walked away from you on your wedding day.

"That's true," she admitted aloud, "but otherwise, Ben was always someone I could depend on—rational, reliable, outgoing, secure in himself, a safe haven, never out of control."

And then there was Tonio, the exact opposite of Ben—volatile, complicated, unpredictable, stubborn, moody, secretive. Not the sort of man who would make a good husband. His mistress would always be his writing. But that didn't make him any less appealing.

Ashley drained her coffee cup and pushed back her chair. She went inside, picked up her thumb-worn Bible, and hugged it to her chest. *Look at you, Ashley. You're getting so caught up in these two men, you're forgetting the real love of your life: Jesus. When you can't figure out what you're supposed to do, just focus on Him. Love Jesus, and God will take care of everything else.*

She returned to the lanai, sat down, and read several chapters of the Gospel of Mark. She loved the verses about loving God with all your heart, soul, mind, and strength. How she yearned to love Him that way. "Instead, I go around acting like a silly, foolish, lovesick girl. I let everything in my life distract me from You, Lord. I get so obsessed with what I want, what I think I need. It's all about me. Forgive me, Jesus. Keep my mind stayed on You. Help me to love You more."

She looked out toward the main house and saw Harry approaching the cottage, a tattered straw hat shading his timeworn face. "Aloha, Harry."

He stooped down and started working on the flower bed by the lanai. "Aloha, sistah."

"How are you doing today?"

"Ev'ryting's jus' fine. Dat nice young man goin' home today?"

"You mean Ben?"

"Yeah, dat's da fella."

"Yes, he's leaving this morning."

"Tell him Harry from da garden sends his aloha."

"I will, Harry. Thanks."

It's true. Ben is going home today, she reflected, *and a part of me wants to go with him. But I can't leave Tonio yet, with only the first draft of his novel finished.*

She looked at her watch. Time for breakfast. She'd better get over to the main house. *And put on a happy face, Ashley, so no one suspects how shaky your emotions are today.*

She entered the dining room just as Ben and Tonio were about to sit down. Ben came around and pulled back her chair, making a gallant flourish as she sat down. "Good morning, milady."

"Thank you, kind sir," she said with forced brightness.

"Good morning, Ashley," said Tonio, eyeing her curiously. "I hope you slept well."

"Very well, thank you." *And I hope you feel guilty for ditching us last night.*

Mika greeted them and poured their coffee.

"Thanks, Mika," said Ben. "Nothing like a cup of strong Kona coffee first thing in the morning. I'm going to miss this back in New York."

"Ben and I had a very pleasant evening last night," Ashley told Tonio. "We sat out on the lanai and watched the most gorgeous sunset."

"And caught up on old times," said Ben. "It was a perfect final evening in Hawaii."

"Of course, it went by too fast," said Ashley. *But not fast enough if you were with some other woman, Tonio.*

"Yes, way too fast," said Ben. "You know, I tried to talk your girl Friday into coming back to New York, but she insists on being true blue to you."

Tonio gave Ashley a pleased glance. "Is that so? I'm glad to hear it. We still have a lot of work to do on the book."

Always the book, thought Ashley. *What about me?*

Ben drummed his fingers on the table. "Well, maybe when the work is done, she'll change her tune. What do you say, Ashley? Is there a chance I'll see you back in New York one of these days?"

"There's always a chance, Ben," she said demurely.

"I'll hold you to that." Ben glanced at his watch. "Looks like it's time to call a taxi."

"Forget the taxi, Ben. Ashley and I can drive you to the airport."

"No need, Tonio. You two have work to do. A quiet taxi ride will give me time to change hats from vacation to work mode."

Tonio chuckled. "If this was your vacation, I'd hate to see what your normal workday looks like."

Ben's gaze flitted to Ashley, then back to Tonio. "The truth is, I thoroughly enjoyed working with you and Ashley on your book. It was a profitable week for all of us."

Ben got up from the table and called for a taxi on his cell phone.

A half hour later, Ashley, keeping watch at the window, spotted the taxi approaching on the circular driveway. "It's here, Ben."

Tonio helped carry Ben's luggage out to the vehicle, then the two shook hands. "Good-bye, ol' man, it's been real," said Ben.

"We'll have to do this again," said Tonio. "On the next book."

"You're on." Ben slapped Tonio's arm then turned to Ashley and opened his arms to her.

Tonio stepped back as Ashley and Ben embraced.

"I'll miss you, Ash," Ben whispered against her cheek. "I meant it about you coming home."

"I can't make any promises, Ben."

"I know. I'm not asking you to. Just remember, I love you."

"I care about you, too, but. . ."

"No buts. I want you back, but it's in God's hands. He'll show you what to do. Just pray about it, okay?"

"I'll be praying for you—that God will bless your life and help you to grow in Him. Good-bye, Ben." She was about to step away when he drew her closer and kissed her soundly on the lips. For a moment she was caught up in the sweet warmth of his touch, his closeness. The rest of the world receded, and they were the only two on earth. Then, suddenly she remembered Tonio was watching. Flustered, she broke away from Ben and stumbled backward. . .into Tonio's arms.

As Tonio steadied her, Ben climbed into the taxi and called back, "Take good care of my girl, Tonio."

Tonio kept his arm firmly around her. "Don't worry, Ben. She's in good hands."

After Ben's taxi disappeared down the road, Tonio looked down at Ashley. "Guess it's time for us to get to work, huh?"

"Yes, I suppose it is."

In silence they walked to the office, took their usual places at his desk, and began going through paperwork. "Do you want me to answer some of your fan mail?" she asked, picking up a stack of unopened letters.

"Sure, go ahead. I'll go over the rewrite of my last chapter."

They began working, but Ashley could tell Tonio's heart was no more into it than hers was. They were both feeling distracted, unmotivated.

After a half hour, Tonio said, "That's it. I'm worthless today."

She pushed the fan letters aside. "Me, too. What's wrong with us?"

Tonio gave her a long, hard look. "I guess there's just way too much going on under the surface."

She gave him a quizzical glance. "What do you mean?"

"You know what I mean."

"No, Tonio, I don't. I can't read your mind, as much as I

would like to at times."

"I'm talking about us, Ashley."

"Us? There is no *us*, except in a very general sense."

He cracked his knuckles. "Well, there should be."

"You're talking in riddles."

"Don't you feel the undercurrent? All the stuff we're feeling that we're not saying? All the emotions we keep pushing away?"

Her mouth went dry. She felt suddenly threatened, exposed. What was Tonio trying to say? Had he guessed how she felt about him? Why in the world was he determined to scrutinize their relationship now when she had just said good-bye to Ben?

"Are you still in love with him?" he asked, his frosty blue eyes drilling into hers.

"In love? You mean, with Ben?"

"Yes, Ben. Who else?"

"I care about him, yes. You know that."

Tonio's brows knitted together; his eyes narrowed. "Are you *in* love with him?"

She broke away from his relentless gaze. Her stomach was churning more now than when Ben had left. "I don't know." Her voice quavered. "That's a question I'm still asking myself."

"He kissed you. You seemed to be enjoying it."

"I'm sorry. I didn't expect him to—he just—"

Tonio waved her off. "I know. You don't have to explain."

She looked back at him. "Then what is this all about?"

Tonio stood up and walked around the room, rubbing his chin. After a minute he sat down on the sofa and patted the spot beside him. "Come sit down. We need to talk."

She looked down at the stack of fan mail.

"Forget the work for now. We have more important things to talk about."

She got up and crossed the room to the sofa. She sat down warily and straightened her teal cotton shirt over her white capris. "Okay, I'm listening."

He combed his fingers through his thick curly hair. "You're not making this easy, Ashley."

"And you're making this—whatever it is—clear as mud. If you have something to say, Tonio, just say it."

He took her hand and wove his fingers between hers.

"What are you doing, Tonio?"

He squeezed her hand tighter. "I feel so awkward in moments like these. I'm a writer and now I can't even put a string of words together. Listen to me—I'm rambling incoherently."

"It's okay. Please, just say what's on your mind."

He swiveled to face her. His tanned, rugged face had never looked more vulnerable. "All right, here's the truth. I love you, Ashley. I adore you. I want you here with me always."

Had she heard right? "You love me?"

"I've loved you since the moment I saw you on the cruise. I've fought it, I've argued with myself, I've told myself you still belong to Ben. It doesn't matter. When I saw him kissing you this morning, I knew I couldn't keep silent another minute. Don't get me wrong. I like and respect Ben. He's a fine man and I'm sure he will make someone a decent husband. But not you. You don't belong with him. You belong with me. Do you hear me, Ashley?"

She sank back against the couch, her mind somersaulting. *This isn't happening. I must be crazy as a loon. Tonio wouldn't say—couldn't possibly say—he loves me!*

He touched her cheek. "I've shocked you, haven't I?"

"No, not at all. I'm just—"

"Shocked?"

She nodded. "Shocked. I don't know what to say."

"Don't say anything. Just let it all sink in."

"It's not sinking in. *I'm* sinking." She tried to stand, but her ankles gave out, so she sat back down.

Tonio sat back and inhaled sharply. "I shouldn't have just blurted it out. I should have built up to it. I've completely unnerved you, haven't I?"

"Maybe a little." She rubbed her stomach. "I do feel a little queasy."

"Are you going to be sick?"

She put her hand over her mouth. "I might."

"Do you want to go back to the cottage?"

"Do you mind?"

"No, not at all. We—we'll talk later."

She nodded, still holding her mouth. He helped her up and walked her to the door. "Are you going to be okay?"

"Yes, I just need to take something to settle my stomach."

"Let me know if you'd like Mika to bring you some tea and toast."

"I will."

She ran back to the cottage. Once inside, she collapsed on her bed, closed her eyes, and tried some slow-breathing exercises. Visions of Tonio danced in her head—his words, his face, his touch. Gradually the frantic images subsided; she was regaining control. After a few minutes her stomach relaxed and her head stopped spinning. Looking up at the ceiling, she said, "Ashley Bancroft, what are you doing? Anthony Adler just told you he loved you, and you as much as told him you had to throw up!"

She sat up on the bed and covered her face with her hands. "What have I done? I just turned an incredibly romantic moment into a travesty, a joke, a charade. Tonio must think I'm an idiot."

She paused and let the silence wash over her. She could feel the tension draining out of her body; her mind was clearing, absorbing what had just happened.

Tonio loves me. A little thrill of delight spiraled through her chest. *He loves me! That's all I need to know. And I love him, too. I have to tell him so.*

She sprang from her bed and went to the mirror to inspect her makeup. She ran a brush through her hair and did a little pirouette to check her outfit. But as she headed for the door, another thought brought her up short. *Hold on, Ashley. No matter what Tonio said, he's a man of mystery, a man with problems, and he's kept secrets from you. You can't let yourself fall in love with a man you don't really know. Didn't you learn from Ben? You can't have a relationship with someone unless he's the man God wants for you.*

"And that's not Tonio, is it, Lord? He's not the one You want for me." She whistled through her teeth. "Why does this keep happening to me? I feel like I'm jumping from the frying pan into the fire. What am I supposed to do now, Lord?"

She walked back to the main house, scouring her mind for the right words. *Tonio, I appreciate you sharing your feelings with me. . . . Tonio, let's just forget what you said and pretend nothing happened. . . . Tonio, I do care about you and want to be friends, but. . .*

"I sound so lame. Help me, Lord. I'm stuck. I don't know what to say or do. It's Your call, Father. Please, please, just let me do the right thing!"

fourteen

This is awkward," said Ashley as she joined Tonio in the dining room for lunch. It had taken every ounce of courage she had to face him again. "I'm sorry I ran out like such a crazy person. I really did think I was going to be sick."

"Don't apologize," said Tonio, pulling back her chair. "I have to admit you looked a bit green around the gills. How are you feeling?"

"A little better. But I think I'll go with the tea and toast you mentioned earlier."

"Good idea. And please let me be the one to apologize."

"Why? You didn't do anything wrong."

"I'm the one who put my foot in my mouth—confronting you with my feelings when you had just said good-bye to Ben."

She sat down. "And I'm the one who nearly upchucked on all your sincere sentiments."

"I'm sure it wasn't deliberate."

"No, but it was totally embarrassing."

He sat down across from her. "Well, since we're both feeling duly chagrined, shall we just call it even?"

She managed a smile. "I'm willing if you are."

He winked. "Maybe we should tell Mika we want humble pie for dessert."

Just then Mika appeared with tuna sandwiches and a fruit salad. "You want humble pie, Mr. Adler? What kind of fruit is that?"

They both laughed. "Maybe fruit of the Spirit," said Tonio. "Never mind, Mika. This will do just fine."

"Just tea and toast for me," said Ashley. "My stomach's a little upset."

Mika's round face clouded with concern. "Is it something you ate?"

"No, Mika. A little too much emotion for one day."

"Yes, I see. You looked sad when Mr. Radison left. He's a very nice man."

"Yes, he is," Ashley agreed, avoiding Tonio's gaze.

Mika smiled. "Mr. Adler, while I get the tea and toast, you cheer up Miss Ashley and make her forget Mr. Radison."

Tonio cast Ashley a knowing grin. "I'm trying, Mika. Believe me, I'm trying."

"I'm fine," Ashley insisted. "Please, both of you stop fussing over me."

"I won't say another word," said Tonio. He put his fingers to his mouth and pretended to turn a key. "My lips are sealed."

"Thank you, kind sir."

Ashley ate her tea and toast in silence, but it did no good. Her thoughts were all over the place. She kept hearing Tonio's words, *"I love you, Ashley. I love you!"* Every time she glanced at him across the table, she felt her face flame. She couldn't pretend nothing had happened between them. Their relationship was different now. Tonio knew it, and so did she.

That afternoon, when they had finished reworking a scene from his novel, Ashley broached the subject that had been weighing on her mind all afternoon. "Tonio, we—we both know there's an elephant in the room."

He nodded. "I know. He's sitting right between us. A pink one. Bright pink. Wearing purple polka dots. And he's laughing. If elephants laugh, that is."

"Stop it, Tonio. Don't make fun of me. You know what I mean. We need to talk about what you said this morning. It's like a neon sign. I can't just ignore it."

"Wonderful. I had my say this morning. Now it's your turn."

She twisted a strand of her hair. "It's not that easy, Tonio. You know I care about you. On some level I suppose I love you. But after my broken romance with Ben, I realize I can't rush ahead of God. I can't force my own agenda. Or follow anyone else's. Only God's. And right now I have no idea what He wants for me. Or for you. I don't know if there could ever be an *us*."

Tonio rubbed his jaw thoughtfully. "I agree, Ashley. Neither of us wants to do anything unless we sense God's approval. All I'm asking is this: Are you willing to pray about it and explore the possibilities?"

"Maybe. In time."

"Why not now?"

She was silent a moment, her folded hands pressed against her lips. Finally she said, "Because there's so much I don't know about you. You're such a private man. I understand that. But people who love each other need to share their hearts, the truth about themselves, the good and the bad."

Tonio stiffened. "What is it you think you need to know about me? What truth are you talking about?"

"I—I need to know. . ." Ashley's mouth went dry, but she forced out the words. "I need to know about your wife."

"You mean, how she died—is that what you want to know?" His tone was mildly accusing.

"Yes, that's part of it," she admitted in a small, breathless voice.

Tonio stood up and paced the room. "Have you read the newspaper accounts?"

When she didn't answer, he repeated the question. "You've read about the accident, haven't you? All the lurid details?"

"Yes, I've read some of the stories. But I need to hear it from you."

He turned to face her, his eyes blazing, his face wrenched with agony. "Hear what? That I killed my wife? It's true. If it wasn't for me, my wife would still be alive!"

⁓

Later, Ashley kicked herself for not insisting that Tonio explain his shocking confession. At the time she had been too stunned to speak. And when he made no effort to clarify his words, she had mumbled something about feeling sick again and fled the room, trembling.

That evening when she joined him for dinner, he acted as if everything were normal, as if he had never uttered such a shattering revelation.

Over the next few days, as they resumed their usual routine of writing and editing, Ashley shuddered at the thought of broaching the subject of Tonio's wife. She never again wanted to see that look of anguish in Tonio's eyes.

Chicken, she chided herself. *You're letting Tonio off too easily. You deserve an answer. Make him tell you what happened.*

But whenever she considered inquiring about the accident, her mouth went dry and her heart pounded furiously. She knew in her heart of hearts that she didn't want to know the truth. It could destroy everything she had ever felt for Tonio.

On Friday evening Tonio didn't show up for dinner. "He went to a meeting in town, Miss Ashley," said Mika. "But he forgot his wallet. He called and asked Harry to take it to him."

"I can do it," said Ashley. "No sense in Harry going out after a hard day of work."

"Harry don't mind."

"No, really, Mika. I'd be glad to take it. Where is Tonio's meeting?"

"The Royal Kona Resort. On Ali'i Drive."

"Great. I'll leave right now. I know Tonio wouldn't want to drive home without his license."

Mika handed her the wallet. "Give it to Mr. Ramiriz. He's at the front desk. Mr. Adler says he will pick it up after his meeting."

"Will do," said Ashley, trying not to sound overly enthusiastic. At last she would have a chance to discover what Tonio was doing at his mysterious meetings.

Guilt nudged her as she made the short drive to the hotel. *What gives you the right to spy on Tonio? It's his business where he goes and what he does. What would he say if he knew you were tracking him down?*

"I'm not tracking him down," she said aloud. "I'm doing him a favor."

Doing yourself a favor, you mean. You've been dying to know where he goes on his secret jaunts.

"What else am I supposed to do? He's the most mystifying man I've ever met!"

She was still arguing with herself as she arrived at the luxurious multi-tiered resort and parked near the entrance. She crossed a lush tropical lagoon to the expansive lobby with its rows of white pillars flanking a tropical garden. Grasping the wallet, she walked the length of the white marble floor until she found the appropriate desk. In her sneakers and jeans, she felt a little like a beggar in a palace. But it was worth it if she could discover what drew Tonio to this place so often. *But what if I don't even see Tonio here? What if I don't learn a thing from this trip?*

"Excuse me. Are you Mr. Ramiriz?" she asked the thin, dark-haired man behind the desk. When he nodded, she held out the wallet. "Mr. Anthony Adler wanted me to deliver this to him. If you could tell me where to find him. . ."

"Thank you, miss. I will give it to him."

"I really don't mind," she murmured, knowing she had already lost the battle. Beady-eyed Mr. Ramiriz wasn't going to tell her a thing. With a sigh of defeat, she relinquished the wallet. Turning to go, she paused to gaze up and down the lobby. Maybe, just maybe, she would spot Tonio among the passing tourists.

As if on cue, her eyes settled on a familiar figure standing near the tiki-style open-air restaurant. Tonio! Ashley was about to cross the room to him when she noticed an attractive, stylishly dressed woman approach him. In her midtwenties, with flowing, platinum blond hair, the woman greeted Tonio and went into his arms as if she belonged there. They embraced for a long moment; then, with his arm comfortably around her waist, he escorted her toward the elevators. Ashley watched as they stepped inside and the doors closed.

Something closed in Ashley's heart, as well. *He has someone else. How can it be? A few days ago he was proclaiming his love for me, but all along he's been having secret rendezvous with another woman!*

Ashley could hardly see to drive home. She kept swatting away hot, angry tears, but more kept coming. *You fool! How could you have trusted a man as devious as Tonio? Finish your work and get back to New York as fast as you can.*

fifteen

Dixie? Dixie Salinger? Where are you, girl? Pick up!" Ashley clutched her cell phone to her ear as if grasping a lifeline. "Come on, Dixie. I need to talk to you, pronto."

Ashley's heart sank when the line went to voice mail. "Sorry I missed your call," came Dixie's lilting, singsong patter. "I'm out skydiving, bungee jumping, or just giving someone a fabulous makeover with my new line of cosmetics. Leave me a message and I'll—" Dixie's voice broke through the recorded message. "Ash, is that you? I'm here!"

Ashley let out a sigh of relief. "Oh, Dixie, am I glad to hear your voice!"

"What's wrong, girl? You sound stressed out."

Ashley sat down on her bed and crossed her legs. "You wouldn't believe what's been happening around here."

"Give me the details," said Dixie.

"I don't even know where to start."

"The beginning works for me."

"Okay, here goes." Ashley drew in a deep breath. "You'll never believe this. Tonio told me he loves me."

"He loves you? Wow! That's amazing. What did you say?"

"Nothing. I almost threw up on him."

Dixie chuckled. "That's probably not the reaction he was looking for."

"I couldn't help it, Dix. My emotions were all over the place. He told me the same day Ben left, right after he kissed me."

"Who kissed you? Tonio?"

"No, Ben."

"Ben kissed you?"

"Yes. Right after he said he wanted to marry me."

"Tonio?"

"No, Ben."

"Ben wants you back?"

"Yes, and when Tonio saw us kissing—"

"Tonio was there?"

"Yes, we were saying good-bye to Ben."

"Listen, girl, my head is spinning."

"Mine is, too, Dixie. I'm so confused."

"Hold on. You're telling me two amazing guys are in love with you?"

"That's only part of it. You haven't heard the rest."

"Something tells me it's not good news."

"It's awful, Dixie." Ashley lay back on her bed and hugged her pillow. "Like something out of one of Tonio's novels."

"Tell me, girl, before curiosity kills this cat."

Ashley searched for the right words. There were none.

"Just spill it," urged Dixie. "It's bad, isn't it?"

"The worst," said Ashley. "It's Tonio. He told me it was his fault his wife died."

Dixie whistled through her teeth. "Wow, I wasn't expecting that."

"Me either. I couldn't believe my ears, Dixie."

"He actually said those words—'it was my fault'?"

"It was something like that. He was responsible. I don't know, Dixie. What does it matter how he said it? He admitted he was to blame."

"How did she die? And are you safe around him? You'd better get on the next plane, girl!"

"Wait, Dixie. I'm running ahead of myself. Tonio's wife died in a car crash." Ashley repeated the grisly details she had gleaned from the Internet stories. "So, you see, it was an accident. But he still feels guilty."

"Whew!" said Dixie. "There's a difference between 'I deliberately killed my wife' and 'I feel guilty that my wife died in a terrible accident.' Did he explain what happened?"

"No. I couldn't bear to hear it. And now I don't know if it matters anyway."

"Why not? You just told me Tonio loves you. So you need to know the truth about his wife."

"There's more," said Ashley.

"More? What more could there be? Your life already sounds like a soap opera."

"Wait 'til you hear this. Tonight I—I saw Tonio with another woman. He's been going to these mysterious meetings in town. I saw them. They looked very cozy together."

"You've got to be kidding!" exclaimed Dixie. "You're making all this stuff up, right, Ash? This is the plot of your next novel."

Ashley sat up and swung her feet off the bed. "I promise you, Dixie, every word is true. I couldn't put all this in a novel. No one would believe it."

"All right, tell me this," said Dixie. "Why would Tonio tell you he loves you if he's seeing another woman? What's the point of that?"

Ashley shook her head. "Like I said, Dixie, nothing makes sense around here."

"Sounds like it's time for you to come home."

"I can't. Not yet. The final rewrite on Tonio's novel isn't finished yet."

"Forget the novel. Just come home."

"I will. Soon." Ashley's voice quavered. "I just wish you were here, Dixie."

"Me, too."

"But I know you wouldn't want to come to Hawaii again so soon." Ashley let the tantalizing idea linger in the air between them like a moth circling a light.

Dixie took the bait. "I wouldn't? Why not? I love doing crazy, unexpected things. I'll be there. I'm catching the next plane to Kona!"

❧

The next morning, when Ashley told Tonio he would be having

another houseguest, she felt a bit guilty for manipulating the situation. It wasn't as if she had twisted Dixie's arm, but she had known just what to say to convince her best friend to come to her rescue.

To Ashley's surprise, Tonio actually seemed pleased that Dixie was coming to visit. "Good for you, Ashley. You've been working so hard, you deserve some relaxation. You girls take a few days off and go have fun."

Why? she challenged silently. *So you can spend more time with your secret love?* Immediately shame flooded her heart, washing away her unspoken accusation. She had no right to condemn Tonio when all she had were suspicions. Maybe Tonio had a good explanation for everything—his wife's death, his elusiveness, his clandestine meetings with the beautiful stranger, his volatile emotions. Surely Dixie would help Ashley put everything into proper perspective.

That afternoon Ashley picked Dixie up at the Kona airport in Tonio's SUV. The two hugged and talked at once, babbling like long-lost friends. "I can't believe it's only been four months since I was in Hawaii," said Dixie as they drove back to Tonio's estate. "It seems like we've been apart for years."

Ashley nodded. "So much has happened, I feel the same way." She glanced over at Dixie. "I like the magenta streaks in your hair. Very spicy."

She tossed her head jauntily. "I got tired of plain auburn."

"I wouldn't care if you showed up bald; I'm thrilled to have you here."

Dixie laughed. "Well, that's a style I hadn't considered." She put her hand out the open window. "I can't believe this is nearly November. It still feels like summer here. You can't imagine how glad I was to have an excuse to leave the drizzly cold of New York."

"Forget the cold weather," said Ashley. "For the next few days you're going to bake in the sun and swim in the pool 'til you're waterlogged."

Dixie clapped her hands in glee. "I can't wait to show all the pale people back home my gorgeous tan!"

As they followed the circular drive to the main house, Dixie let out a whistle. "Don't tell me, Ashley! *This* is where you've been hanging out for the past few months? Talk about living in the lap of luxury!"

Ashley nodded. "Sweet, isn't it? Sometimes when I wake up in the morning, I think I must be dreaming, it's so beautiful around here. Tomorrow I'll show you around the estate."

"So tell me the truth," said Dixie. "Is Tonio bummed that I'm intruding on his privacy?"

"Not at all," said Ashley. "He seems quite pleased that you're visiting. In fact, in spite of everything that's happened, he acts like things are perfectly normal. It's infuriating."

"Well, let's see how things look to this objective bystander. Okay, so I'm not so objective. But at least I'll give you my honest opinion."

"That's what I need, Dixie. Someone with a clear head and discerning spirit."

Dixie chuckled. "That's me, all right. A regular eagle-eyed Sherlock Holmes."

That evening Mika pulled out all the stops and served a lavish seafood dinner of salmon pâte, fried calamari, and shrimp curry with cashews and mango chutney.

"Dixie, I hope you like fish," said Tonio. "These dishes are Mika's specialties. They're out of this world. Right, Ashley?"

"Absolutely!" She passed the salmon pâte and curry to Dixie.

"It's delicious, Mika," said Dixie, sampling the pâte. "If I didn't like seafood before, I do now."

"Save room," urged Mika. "There's passion fruit and macadamia nut pie for dessert."

Dixie licked her lips. "Given half a chance, I could learn to eat like this every day. It sure beats my usual frozen pizza and boxed macaroni and cheese."

Everyone laughed.

"What's so funny?" said Dixie with a shrug. "What's more American than pizza and macaroni?"

"American or not, we're skipping your old favorites this week," said Ashley. "With Mika cooking, you're going to get the best Hawaiian cuisine anywhere."

Dixie helped herself to more curry. "Girl, you may have to roll me onto the plane when it's time to go."

❧

Over the next few days Ashley and Dixie behaved like typical tourists—driving around Kona, seeing all the sights Dixie had missed on her cruise ship visit, shopping, snorkeling, swimming, and sunbathing around the pool. They visited museums and historic sites until they doubted they could cram another bit of island trivia into their brains. Tonio joined them one day for a kayaking excursion through the rain forest—"*flumin da ditch*," as he called it—and a whale-watching cruise the next day. It was all good fun. But most of all, Ashley and Dixie relished their private, late-night gabfests in her little cottage.

"I feel like a teenager again," said Ashley one evening as they curled up on her bed with sodas and brimming bowls of popcorn.

"Remember all the slumber parties we used to have," said Dixie, "when we'd stay up 'til dawn laughing and talking?"

"And lamenting our latest boyfriend crises," mused Ashley.

"Oh, yes! The boyfriend crises. Was there ever *not* a crisis?"

"Never! We always thought it was the end of the world. Life would never be the same without—whoever."

Dixie rolled her soda can between her palms. "We've come a long way, girlfriend. Look at us, sitting here in this exotic estate, with the ocean just a stone's throw away. How great is this?"

"And we're still lamenting our boyfriend problems! What's with that?"

"Some things never change," said Dixie.

Ashley tossed a kernel of corn, hitting Dixie's nose. "Since you got here, I've done all the talking. What about you, Dix? There must be some special guy in your life."

Dixie shrugged. "Not so much. Lots of buddies, but no one special."

"You're not seeing anyone?"

"Not really. I have guy friends. We hang out once in a while. That's all. But I'm content. I don't know if I could handle the drama of a relationship right now."

"You mean, like I'm going through with Tonio?"

"Exactly. So we're back to Tonio."

"Afraid so," agreed Ashley, sitting back on the bed. "And you still haven't told me what you think. You've had a chance to observe him these past few days. What's your opinion?"

"I think he's crazy about you. But he's a hard one to figure out. He doesn't let anyone see the real guy under all the charm and swagger."

"I can't get him to talk about himself," said Ashley. "But then again, I'm not very good at drawing him out. I guess I'd rather not know the bad things."

"You won't know if he's right for you until you take off those rose-colored glasses."

"I know. I just wish the Lord would give me some direction."

"I'm sure you've been praying about it."

"Of course." Ashley twisted a strand of hair around her finger. "But sometimes I feel like I'm just giving God a shopping list. 'Give me this, Lord, give me that. Make Tonio fall in love with me. Make everything perfect for us.' It sounds so selfish, doesn't it, Dixie?"

"It sounds *human*. I do that, too. I think we all do. It's the natural thing to do."

"I don't want to be satisfied with a faith that's always saying 'give me.' I want to grow closer to God, but I get so caught up in all the other things—Tonio, his book, our daily routine, my feelings for him. I hate to say it, but sometimes God is an afterthought."

Dixie nodded. "Every day is a new chance to show Jesus how much we love Him. But sometimes I get halfway through the day before I even think of Him."

Ashley grimaced. "Doesn't sound like we're doing too well spiritually, are we?"

"We could pray right now," said Dixie.

"I'd like that," said Ashley. "Remember the Bible verse about God's strength being made perfect in weakness? Well, God can have a field day with all my weaknesses."

"Stand in line, Ash. I've probably got you beat by a mile."

They both laughed. "We'll let God sort it out," said Dixie.

They took turns praying conversationally, expressing their gratitude and making requests or sitting in companionable silence for a few moments of private worship. After awhile Dixie began singing a familiar chorus and Ashley joined in. When they had finished they both had tears rolling down their cheeks.

"This is like the old days," said Ashley.

"It sure is," said Dixie. "Remember how we'd both be a mess emotionally? Upset about one thing or another. But after we prayed together, everything looked different. God felt so close. I miss those days."

"Me, too."

Dixie squeezed Ashley's hand. "I have a feeling God's going to do something amazing in the next few days."

"I feel it, too," said Ashley. "Things are going to change in a big way. I just pray I'm ready for whatever happens."

"You will be, Ash. God is with us, and He never fails."

Ashley nodded. "I just pray I won't fail Him."

❧

The next day, after Ashley and Dixie returned home from an afternoon of shopping, they found Tonio in his office, at his desk, dressed in a tan sport jacket. He was talking on the phone, speaking in hushed tones. "It's still the Royal Kona Resort. But it's a different room, Lydia. The Empire Room.

That's right. I'll see you shortly."

When he looked up and saw Ashley and Dixie standing there, he said a quick good-bye and hung up the receiver. He looked like a man who had been found out.

He was talking with her—that woman at the hotel! Ashley realized with a sinking sensation.

He stood up and said, almost too brightly, "Well, look who's home. Looks like you girls had a great day shopping."

They set their packages on the sofa. "I'm sorry, Tonio," said Ashley, fighting her disappointment. "We didn't mean to interrupt."

"No problem. I was finished talking anyway." He strode over and gazed down at their purchases. "So did you get some great buys? If I remember right, Dixie, you went home with half of Hawaii the last time you were here."

"I sure did. And this time I got the other half."

"Terrific. What did you girls buy?"

Ashley let Dixie do the talking. "I bought some more of those plastic plumeria leis for my cosmetics customers, some limited edition lithographs of the ocean for my apartment, a conch shell for my bathroom shelf, and, of course, more Kona coffee."

"What about you, Ashley?" asked Tonio. "What did you buy?"

"Some clothes. Nothing important." She kept her gaze fixed on him. "You're dressed up tonight. Are you going out?"

"I have a meeting tonight."

"Then you won't be here for dinner?"

"No, afraid not. But I won't be out late."

"It doesn't matter." Ashley gathered up her purchases and said a curt good-bye to Tonio. With a little wave, Dixie scooped up her packages and followed Ashley back to the cottage.

"I can't believe it," Ashley lamented as she tossed her purchases on the bed. "He's going to the resort to be with that woman! And after I prayed so hard last night."

Dixie set her bags on the chair. "As I remember it, Ash, you asked God to do things His way, not yours."

"Whose side are you on anyway?" Ashley shot back.

"There's only one side that matters, and that's God's."

Ashley sat down on the bed and wiped away an offending tear. "I know you're right, Dixie, but right now I just want to wallow in my misery."

Dixie sat down beside her. "What can I do to help?"

"There's nothing anyone can do. I just wish I knew what was going on. Why doesn't he come right out and tell me he's found someone else? Then I could accept it and move on. It's the not knowing that's killing me."

"You could ask him."

"No, I can't. I get tongue-tied just thinking about it."

"Then you're going to have to leave it with the Lord."

"I'm trying, but. . ." Ashley paused. "Wait a minute. He told her he's meeting her in the Empire Room at the Royal Kona Resort. We could go there, Dixie."

"Go there? You mean spy on them?"

"Not spy exactly. Just take a peek inside and see what's happening."

"Ash, I'm usually the first to try some new adventure. But this would be wrong."

"Why? It's surely not a private hotel room. It sounds like a conference room. Anyone can probably go in."

"I still don't have a good feeling about it," said Dixie.

"You said you wanted to help me. Come with me, Dixie. I don't want to do this alone."

Dixie shook her head. "I'll go, but I hope we don't regret it."

"How can we regret it? If I get some answers about Tonio, it'll be a good thing."

Ashley was still telling herself that as they drove Tonio's other car—a blue sedan—to the Royal Kona Resort. They parked near the entrance, made their way into the lobby, and checked the hotel directory for the Empire Room.

"It's on the second floor," said Ashley.

As they headed for the elevators, Dixie whispered, "Are you sure you want to do this?"

"We've come this far. I've got to know."

They took the elevator to the second floor, got off, and walked down the hall past several conference rooms. At last they came to the Empire Room. The door was closed.

"It's not too late to turn back," Dixie whispered.

"No way!" Quietly Ashley turned the knob and opened the door a crack. She could see people inside the room. She opened the door wider and stepped inside. Thirty or more people sat in a semicircle facing the front. The blond on the far right was the woman Tonio had met in the lobby, the woman he had called *Lydia*.

Ashley's eyes were drawn to a tall man standing up and taking the microphone. It was Tonio. What was he doing? Giving a speech?

He cleared his throat, then spoke, his booming baritone sounding loud and clear in the high-ceilinged room. "Good evening, everyone. My name is Tonio. . .and I'm an alcoholic."

sixteen

Just as Tonio said the words, "I'm an alcoholic," his gaze flitted to the back of the room, to the doorway where Ashley and Dixie stood. The moment his eyes met Ashley's, everything in his face changed. He looked stunned, incredulous, betrayed.

Her heart wrenched at the shock and pain in his eyes. She pivoted on her heel and ran from the room, Dixie right behind her. They hurried out to the car and headed home, Ashley sobbing her regrets.

"Why didn't he tell me, Dixie? I never would have gone there tonight if I'd known he was at an AA meeting. How can he be an alcoholic? I never saw him drink, not once."

"He must have known he didn't dare drink," said Dixie, "or he'd be a slave to it again."

"He's carried that burden all this time, and he never told me about it. Why didn't he tell me?"

"Maybe because you put him on a pedestal. He didn't want you to know he was a mere man with weaknesses like anyone else."

Ashley sat forward, trying to see the road through her tears. "I thought I knew him, Dixie. But I don't know him at all!"

"Watch the road, Ash. Want me to drive?"

Ashley blinked back her tears. "No, I'm okay. But I've ruined everything with Tonio. He'll never want to see me again."

"Yes, he will. You'll get through this. Watch that curve, Ashley. It's a steep drop to the ocean below."

The vehicle veered onto the shoulder of the narrow road and skidded, spewing gravel everywhere. The tires squealed as Ashley turned the wheel sharply and got the car back on the pavement. Her heart pounded as she gasped, "Sorry."

Dixie was holding on for dear life. "I said I'd drive."

"I'm okay. We're almost home."

"That's a relief. Are you going to wait up for Tonio?"

"Are you kidding? I couldn't bear to face him tonight."

"You're going to have to face him sometime."

"Tomorrow. After I've had time to get my bearings and summon some courage." Ashley heaved a sigh. "I don't know whether to be angrier with Tonio or myself. He didn't trust me enough to reveal his true self to me. I didn't trust him enough to accept his desire for privacy. We're a fine pair, aren't we?"

Dixie nodded. "I'd say the relationship needs some work. But maybe now you can take things to a new level of trust."

"Thanks, Dixie. You always manage to see the silver lining in every disaster. But I think it's too late for Tonio and me. I think that ship has sailed."

"Maybe, maybe not. We prayed about it last night. Let's wait and see what God's going to do."

When they got back to the cottage, Ashley went straight to bed. At least if she was asleep, she wouldn't be seeing that look of devastation on Tonio's face. But she was wrong. Her dreams were filled with Tonio announcing he was an alcoholic and then staring her down with those sad, wounded, accusing eyes.

The next morning Ashley slept in. When Dixie woke her and said it was time for breakfast, Ashley told her to go on without her. "I hardly slept a wink last night. Tell Mika I'll get something later."

"No way," said Dixie. "If you're not going to breakfast, I'm certainly not going to face Tonio alone. We'll both stay here and have coffee and whatever I can find in the cupboards to snack on."

"You'll find some stale granola cereal, half a grapefruit, and a few brown bananas."

"Okay. That's a start."

But by lunchtime Ashley knew she couldn't hide out in the

cottage any longer. She had no choice but to march over to the main house and face Tonio. Look him straight in the eye and take her punishment. And then give him a taste of his own medicine. Insist on knowing why he kept something so important from her for so long. Did he think she wouldn't understand? Then again, she *didn't* understand. How could Tonio be an alcoholic?

The question still weighed on Ashley's mind as she and Dixie entered the dining room and greeted Mika and Tonio. Mika was serving bowls of fresh fruit and tuna salad sandwiches. Tonio was in his usual spot, reading the newspaper. When they took their seats, he put his paper down and gave them a thin smile. "We missed you at breakfast," he said.

"We slept in," said Dixie.

"Not good to skip breakfast," said Mika, filling their glasses with iced tea.

"We had breakfast in the cottage," said Ashley. *Stale cereal and overripe bananas.*

Tonio cleared his throat. "When I saw you girls at my meeting last night, I thought there must have been an emergency at home. But Mika assured me everything was all right."

"About your meeting, Tonio," said Ashley, lowering her gaze. "I'm sorry. We shouldn't have barged in like that. It was all my idea. I hope you'll forgive me."

"I still don't understand what you were doing there, Ashley."

She stole a sideways glance at Dixie, but Dixie's look said, *You're on your own here, girl!*

"I don't know what to say, Tonio," said Ashley, her throat tightening. "It's just that you were gone so often to your mysterious meetings, I—I was dying to know where you were going. But you never said a word. And then last night I heard you on the phone talking to someone named Lydia, and you mentioned the Empire Room at the Royal Kona Resort. So, on a lark, Dixie and I decided to. . .to—"

"Spy on me?"

"Something like that."

"Let me get this straight," said Tonio, his brows lowering. "You thought I was having a secret tryst with someone named Lydia? And you wanted to find out what was going on?"

She nodded.

"You thought I was having a romantic fling?"

Ashley picked at her tuna salad. "I didn't know."

"How could you think that, Ashley? Especially after I just told you how I felt about you."

Tears welled in her eyes. "I'm sorry."

They all ate in silence for a moment.

Finally Tonio said, "For your information, Ashley, Lydia is a longtime friend. We've both battled the same demon. She got me started in AA when my life was falling apart. I'll forever indebted to her. I care about her, just as I care about her husband and children. But there's no romance."

"I'm sorry, Tonio," Ashley said through her tears. "I didn't know. I feel so stupid."

He handed her his handkerchief. "Don't cry about it. I hate to see a woman cry."

In her most lilting voice, Dixie said, "Did you hear it's snowing in New York? Imagine! We're sitting here in all this sunshine, and—"

"It's my fault, too," Tonio broke in.

Ashley dried her eyes. "Your fault?"

He put down his fork. "I should have told you I was going to AA meetings. I tried to several times, but I couldn't bear to tarnish your image of me."

"All I wanted was to know the real you."

"All right, that's what you're going to do." He tossed his napkin on his plate. "Are you finished eating?"

"Almost. Why?"

"We're going for a long walk and having an even longer talk. You're going to hear it all, Ashley. Every last detail of my life. And we'll see how you feel about me then."

"I'm ready," she said, pushing back her plate.

Tonio stood up and pulled her chair out. As she stood, she glanced over at Dixie.

"Hey, don't worry about me," Dixie said quickly. "You two go off and have fun. I'll stay here and help Mika with the dishes."

"Where do you want to go?" Tonio asked as they left the main house. "The woods, the orchards, the beach?"

"The beach." As she fell into step beside him, a cool breeze rustled her apple-green sundress. Tonio held her hand as they descended the rocky slope to the beach. She removed her sandals as they walked across the sand to a smooth outcropping of rocks near the ocean. He climbed up, then offered his hand and pulled her up beside him. They were close enough to the water to feel the salt spray when the surf came in, surging over the rocky ledge below them. Yet the water was clear enough to see the ocean floor and large sea turtles washing in with the current and back out again.

They both leaned back against the rocks and gazed at the fleecy clouds stretching from Kailua Bay to the edge of Mauna Loa in the far distance.

"This is beautiful," said Ashley. "And so peaceful. Why haven't we come here before?"

"I'm wondering the same thing," said Tonio. "We get so busy with our lives we can't see beyond our own noses. But a view like this really makes you stop and appreciate God's world."

"It does," she agreed. "It kind of puts our little problems in perspective, doesn't it?"

Tonio rubbed his jaw, his lips firmly set. Ashley studied his sturdy, bronzed profile. A faint stubble of beard covered his sculpted chin, and the salty breeze ruffled his sable hair. He looked like a man who wasn't ready to talk.

"We don't have to do this," she murmured. "You don't owe me any explanations. We can just enjoy the ocean and go back home."

He looked at her, his blue eyes gleaming like crystal in the sunlight. "Don't give me a way out, Ashley. I've tried to summon the courage to do this for months now. I want you to know everything."

"Okay. I'm listening."

He crossed his arms on his chest and put his head back. "I met Brianna at a media party just after my first book was made into a movie. She was a press agent and wanted to represent me. She had all these big plans for making me a star, even though writers don't typically end up in the limelight like actors and musicians.

"Anyway, I admired her energy and enthusiasm. I felt flattered that she was willing to take me on as a client when she already had some big-name actors in her stable. One thing led to another and we decided to get married. I suppose it was her idea, but I figured I'd achieved a good measure of success. The one thing missing was a wife."

"It sounds like you made a good team," said Ashley. "You had someone in your corner fighting for you."

Tonio's jaw tightened. "That's what I thought. At first. But when the movie studio passed on the option for one of my books, Brianna was outraged. Coming from a wealthy family, she loved all the trappings of fame—the luxury homes and cars, the travel, the fancy parties, and gala events. She insisted we build this estate with all its pricey amenities. She wasn't happy unless my books were on the best-seller lists. She kept after me to produce another hit, then complained about being bored when I spent long hours writing. She threw herself back into her own career, taking on more clients than she could handle. She was rarely home. She had no time for me or my writing."

Ashley shook her head. "I had no idea, Tonio. I thought Brianna was the love of your life."

He managed a dry chuckle. "The love of my life? Ha! I didn't have a clue what love was all about. Whatever Brianna and I shared, it wasn't love."

"I didn't think anyone could measure up to what you felt for her."

"I'm not proud of my feelings," Tonio admitted. "I hated what our lives had become, and I think she did, too. I started drinking heavily. I had never been a drinking man, but alcohol became an escape. I didn't realize what a destructive power it held until I was caught in its vise grip."

"What about the accident?" Ashley probed gently.

Tonio massaged his knuckles until they were bone white. "Not a day goes by that I don't relive that horrific night."

"If it's too painful, you don't have to talk about it."

He looked at her, his eyes glinting with torment. "Do you think keeping silent has diminished the pain?"

"I suppose not."

"The accident happened on the road along the cliffs near here. It was over five years ago, but I remember it as if it were yesterday." Tonio picked up a pebble and tossed it into the water. "I'd finally optioned another book, and it had been made into a movie. Brianna and I were attending a celebration party at a private estate south of Kona.

"The evening started out well enough. Brianna was excited about the release of the movie. She was sure I was going to be on top again—an A-list celebrity. All I could think of was how badly they had butchered my novel. I was in no mood for a party. If we had just stayed home that night. . ."

"But you didn't."

"No, we didn't," Tonio conceded. "As soon as I got there, I started drinking. I wanted to drink myself into oblivion. I knew the movie would propel me into the spotlight again, and Brianna wouldn't be content until we had exhausted every media opportunity. All I wanted to do was stay home and write. All Brianna wanted to do was surf the crowd and play every publicity angle.

"Finally, I'd had enough. I told her I was going home, and

she was going with me. She refused. We practically had a knock-down, drag-out fight right there in front of everyone. Finally I stalked out to the car and she ran after me. I climbed in the driver's seat, but she wouldn't let me shut the door. She kept telling me to get out and let her drive."

Tonio shifted his torso and lowered his chin to his chest. His voice came out in a hoarse whisper. "Brianna hated driving. Especially at night. Especially on the narrow, winding roads by the cliffs. But she knew I was drunk and couldn't drive. Finally I gave in and let her get behind the wheel. But all the way home we kept arguing. I don't remember now what we said, but the atmosphere was heated, explosive. Neither of us was paying attention to the road."

Tonio paused, his breathing labored. Ashley put her hand on his arm and waited.

After a moment he cleared his throat and squared his shoulders. "I don't remember exactly what happened next. I just know somehow our car veered off the road, crashed through the guardrail, and plunged over the cliff into the ocean below. The whole thing was surreal—the car hitting the water, slowly sinking, water pouring in through the open sunroof, and finally the jarring sensation as we hit the ocean floor. As the car flooded, I held my breath, undid my seat belt, and reached for Brianna. She was unconscious. I tried to pull her free, but she was wedged in against the steering wheel. When I couldn't hold my breath any longer, I forced my way up through the sunroof against the inrush of water. I swam to the surface, took in all the air I could, then dove back down for Brianna.

"By the time I dislodged her from the car and swam with her to shore, I could hardly breathe. I tried CPR, but it was too late. She was gone."

Ashley squeezed Tonio's arm. "I'm so sorry."

With his fingertips he rubbed the moisture from his eyes. "If I hadn't been so drunk, maybe I could have saved her. My mind would have been clearer, my reactions faster. And if I hadn't been drinking in the first place, the crash never would have happened. It was my fault, Ashley. I killed Brianna as surely as if I'd strangled her with my own hands."

"Tonio, you can't blame yourself."

"Who else can I blame?"

"It was an accident."

"An accident that never needed to happen." He looked at her with imploring eyes. "I'll never forgive myself, Ashley. Never! I should have died, not Brianna!"

seventeen

Where is God in all of this?" asked Ashley.

"What do you mean?" said Tonio.

The tide was coming in around them, frothy waves crashing below the rocky ledge where they sat. The sun was lowering, and the breeze had picked up and turned cool.

Shivering, Ashley replied, "You sound like a man without hope."

Tonio reached for her hand, intertwining his fingers with hers. "I don't mean to sound that way. I do have faith. Since the accident I've come to know Christ in a personal way. Even though I was raised in the church and have been a believer most of my life, I took my faith for granted. Having a personal walk with God wasn't my priority. But after the accident I reexamined everything in my life, and I hated what I saw. I threw myself on God's mercy and begged Him to help me stop drinking. He did. He led me to AA. The Lord and AA have kept me sober ever since. But to this day I still struggle with my guilt over Brianna. It shadows every emotion and robs me of the joy I know I should feel in Christ."

"Have you prayed about it? Asked God to forgive you?"

"Every day. But I can't forgive myself. I don't know how to turn off the guilt. A voice in my head keeps accusing me, reminding me I have no right to enjoy such a good life when I robbed Brianna of hers."

"You can't change the past. You can't bring Brianna back."

"I know. I guess that's why I feel so helpless. There's nothing I can do to redeem myself."

"God's the only One who can redeem any of us, Tonio."

He nodded. "I know you're right. But I can't seem to exorcise those demons of the mind that keep reminding me of my guilt. It sounds crazy, I know—I shouldn't even be telling you this—but it's as if the devil himself keeps drawing me to the cliff and taunting me to jump into the ocean to make atonement for my sin; it's as if the only way I'll ever be at peace is to die the way she died."

Ashley stared up at him. "Don't even think such a thing! You're letting the devil's lies destroy you!"

Tonio shook his head. "I knew I shouldn't have said anything. You must think I'm ready for the loony bin."

"I'd never think that. But I am frightened for you."

He squeezed her hand. "Don't worry, I'm not going to do anything drastic. I'm too chicken to go stepping off cliffs. I just wanted to be completely honest with you about how I feel sometimes."

They were both silent for a moment, gazing out at the sea.

Finally Ashley said, "We all have things in our past we regret. We're all just sinners saved by grace. I wish I knew my Bible better. There's a verse in Romans, I think, that says there's no condemnation for those who are in Christ Jesus. While we were still sinners, Christ died for us. We're under grace, Tonio, not guilt."

He smiled. "I know, Ashley. God loves us unconditionally. And that's a beautiful thing."

"Exactly. There's nothing we can do to diminish His love for us, because He loved us when we were already sinners."

"You're preaching to the choir, sweetheart." He brushed his fingers across her cheek. "I believe everything you've said. Nothing can separate us from the love of God. . .except maybe our own guilt. Who knows? Maybe the devil's greatest tool against Christians is to spoil our fellowship with God by making us feel guilty."

"It's true."

"But what if we feel guilty because we *are* guilty?"

She swiveled to face him. "Tonio, may I make an observation?"

"Go on. I'd like to hear this."

"I think I know the answer to your problem."

He managed a curious smile. "My problem? You have the answer?"

Retrieving her hand from his, she drew in a deep breath, gathering her courage. "Your problem is. . ."

"I'm listening."

"It's your pride. The problem is your pride."

"My pride?" His eyes widened. "Okay, little lady, how did you get to that conclusion?"

"It just came to me." She marched her fingers along his arm. "You're one of those macho men, a rugged individualist, captain of his own destiny, who insists on doing everything himself, right?"

"I don't know if I'd use those words, but. . .okay, so what if I am?"

Her hand rested on his wrist. "I remember something my mom used to tell me. If you tell a woman a problem, she'll offer comfort and sympathy. If you tell a man a problem, he'll immediately try to fix it. That's what you're doing, Tonio. Trying to fix your life on your own terms, atone for your sins in your own strength."

He chuckled. "You amaze me. One minute you're an aspiring preacher, the next you're an armchair psychologist."

"I know I'm saying it badly, but someone has to get through to you." She thought a minute, searching for the right words. "It's like salvation. It's not as if we start the process by doing something good, and then God notices and finishes the job. Nothing we do can start the act of redemption. It begins and ends with God. All we can do is acknowledge our unworthiness and accept His grace."

Tonio slipped his arm around her shoulder. "You're actually quite eloquent at times, Ashley."

"Really? You think so?"

"Of course. My admiration for you just keeps increasing."

She shivered again. "You're teasing me, aren't you?"

"No, my darling. I am deeply touched by your concern."

She met his gaze squarely. "The truth is, I care about you, Tonio. It breaks my heart to see you in such pain."

He grinned. "I guess you're an amateur nurse, too, because I'm feeling better already." He drew her closer and rubbed her bare arm. "You're getting chilled. Maybe we'd better head back to the house."

"I suppose so."

"But first—we've had such a special time together, Ashley— I'd like to thank the Lord for it."

She smiled. "I'd like that."

He cleared his throat and gazed out at the sea. "Father, thank You for bringing Ashley into my life. In spite of my stubborn, prideful heart, You've blessed me in so many ways. And one of the best blessings is this darling girl who keeps me on my toes and makes me take a hard, honest look at myself. Help me to be the man she believes I can be. I know I can't do it by myself. It's up to You, Lord. Thanks for all You're going to do in both our lives—by the grace of Jesus, amen."

"Amen," Ashley whispered.

Tonio scrambled to his feet, pulled her up beside him, then helped her navigate the rocky shoal back to the wet sand. She slipped her sandals on, and they walked back to the house arm in arm.

As they climbed the steps to the wraparound porch, his grip tightened on her arm. He turned her shoulders to face him and searched her eyes. "Ashley, I can't tell you what it means to me to get this whole thing about my past off my chest and know you don't hate me."

She touched his cheek. "I could never hate you, Tonio."

He leaned down and lightly kissed her lips. "I love you, Ashley."

"I love you, too." Had she actually said those words? Tonio looked as surprised as she was.

"You do? You love me?"

Her face flamed. "Yes. I do."

"That's the best medicine yet!"

She moved her fingertips over his chin. "I'll be praying for you tonight. I pray you'll stop condemning yourself long enough to hear God's voice and feel His love."

He pulled her into his arms and held her so tight, she gasped. He smoothed back her windblown hair and whispered into her ear, "If anyone can help me hear His voice again, it's you, Ashley."

⁂

At dinner that evening Tonio was in the best of moods—talkative, happy, relaxed. As Mika served grilled porterhouse steaks and baked potatoes, he and Ashley exchanged private smiles across the table. Once or twice she was afraid she would succumb to a fit of giggles. As Dixie chatted about her afternoon shopping spree with Mika, Ashley replayed that magical moment when she told Tonio she loved him. The two of them shared a delicious secret—a blossoming love that made her feel downright giddy. She wanted to shout her feelings to the rooftop but refrained, in case Tonio intended to keep their budding romance confidential for now.

While they were still eating dessert, the phone rang. Mika answered and brought the phone to Tonio. "It's Mr. Ben Radison," she announced.

With a grin, Tonio took the receiver and put it on speakerphone. "Hey, Ben, we're all here. Say hello to Ashley and Dixie. We're having a great time. Wish you were here, ol' man. Or then again, maybe not."

"This isn't a call I wanted to make, Tonio." Ben's voice sounded heavy, strained. "But I've got to give you the heads-up."

Tonio grew serious. "What's going on, Ben?"

"You know we put out a lot of advance publicity on your new book. It's been great for presales."

"That's good news. Why so glum?"

"All the publicity has generated some action among the tabloids. I thought you'd better hear it from me."

"Hear what?"

"That network tabloid show that digs up all the dirt on celebrities is doing a retrospective on you. They're dredging up the accident, doing an investigative report, asking, 'Whatever happened to Brianna Adler, beautiful wife of best-selling author Anthony Adler?' I saw it here on New York time; it'll be coming on your TV in a few minutes."

After a long moment of silence, Tonio said, "Thanks for letting me know, Ben." He hung up the phone, strode to the great room, and turned on the television set. As Ashley joined him on the sofa, she could read the tension and submerged fury in his face. The air was charged with an aura of foreboding. Mika disappeared, busying herself in the kitchen. Dixie quietly excused herself and went back to the cottage.

This is bad, Ashley kept thinking. *Really bad!* Her heart pounded as a long string of commercials gave way to the offending tabloid show. Photos and film clips of Tonio and Brianna flashed on the screen as a resonant voice-over declared, "Was Brianna Adler's death really an accident? Or was something more sinister at play here? In spite of his denials, speculation still runs rampant as to whether Anthony Adler was driving the car that killed his wife that fateful autumn night five years ago. Is it possible this renowned author has gotten away with murder?"

The program droned on with its scathing commentary. "Reclusive author Anthony Adler has been out of the spotlight in recent years, but with the literary world already buzzing over his soon-to-be-released novel, long-buried questions about his wife's tragic death have resurfaced."

Ashley cast a sidelong glance at Tonio. His face was livid, the tendons in his neck taut. His fingernails dug into the sofa arm. "Why did I ever think I could wake up from this nightmare?" he muttered under his breath.

At one point the reporter acknowledged a medical examiner's report that confirmed Brianna's chest injuries were consistent with the impact of the steering wheel. "Tonio, that proves you weren't driving," said Ashley.

He nodded. "That was proved from the beginning, but no one paid any attention. The media would rather distort and sensationalize a story than present the facts."

He was right. The reporter was already suggesting that the medical examiner might have been involved in a cover-up, but then added, almost as an afterthought, "So far there has been no evidence of any impropriety."

"You see that?" said Tonio. "They say just enough to put doubt in people's minds, then cover themselves by admitting there's no real evidence to back up their claims."

Ashley clasped his arm. "You know the truth, Tonio, and I know the truth. The people who matter know the truth. That's what counts."

Tonio stood up and turned off the TV, then paced the room. "The truth is, I still feel responsible for Brianna's death. The reporters are right. No matter how you juggle the facts, if it wasn't for me, Brianna would still be alive!"

"Are you saying you had more power over Brianna's life than God did?" countered Ashley. "Tonio, none of us has that kind of power. It's in God's hands who lives and who dies. Every day we live is an undeserved gift from Him."

Tonio waved her off. "Don't, Ashley. No more sermons, please!"

She got up, went to him, and took his hands in hers. "Okay, no more sermons. But listen, Tonio. Forget about that sleazy program. Forget about the past. Concentrate on today, the good things, the special time we had at the beach."

He turned away, his tone brusque. "I can't, Ashley. I need to be alone. Do you mind?"

She pulled him back. "Are you sure? You look like you could

use a friendly face right now."

He looked down at her, his brow furrowed, his eyes blazing. "Please, leave me alone! Go back to the cottage!"

Ashley ran from the room in tears. At the moment, she hated the infuriating Anthony Adler as much as she loved him.

eighteen

When Ashley arrived back at the cottage, she found Dixie sitting cross-legged on the bed, working on her laptop. She looked up and asked, "How's it going, Ash?"

"Don't ask." Ashley walked over to the bureau, picked up her brush, and ran it through her hair. Her lower lip was trembling. She didn't want Dixie to see she was about to burst into tears.

But Dixie knew her all too well. She set her laptop aside, scooted off the bed, and approached with a gentle, "I *am* asking. Talk to me, Ash. Tell me what happened."

The two sat down side by side on the bed. "It was awful, Dixie." Between sobs, Ashley poured out the whole story—her conversation with Tonio on the beach, the loving words they had shared, the joy she felt being with him at dinner, and then his explosive reaction to the tabloid show's accusations. "The way he spoke to me tonight, telling me to leave him alone—it was almost as if he wanted me to hate him, as if he was trying to drive me away. Why would he do that when I just told him I loved him?"

"Maybe he realizes things are getting too serious," said Dixie. "He's probably afraid of making another commitment after what happened with his wife."

"He's making me afraid, too. I never know what to expect from him. What should I do?"

"I hate to say this, Ash, but maybe it's time to go home."

Ashley gave Dixie a questioning glance. "You think so?"

Dixie shrugged. "It has to be your decision, but if you want to know how I see it. . ."

"I do. You always have a way of seeing the truth about things."

"Okay. The way I see it, you've gotten so emotionally involved in Tonio's problems, it's distracting you from your own life, maybe even affecting your walk with the Lord."

Ashley was silent for a long moment before replying, "I suppose you're right. I've been anxious and upset over what's happening with Tonio. I guess that means I'm not really trusting God for the future."

Dixie squeezed Ashley's shoulder. "There's nothing more you can do here to help Tonio. Think about getting on with your own life."

Ashley stifled another sob. "I want to, but I can't leave him like this. He's hurting so much. How can I just walk away?"

"I know it won't be easy, but you can do it. You have to think of yourself now, Ash. Tell me, how long before you're finished editing his novel?"

Ashley picked up her pillow and hugged it against her chest. "I'll finish the final edit in a couple of days. Then it's off to the publisher."

"That's about the time I'm going home," said Dixie. "Why don't you fly home with me?"

Ashley pressed her cheek against the down-feathered pillow. Visions of Tonio's tormented blue eyes lingered in her mind like remnants of a dream. "I can't promise anything, but I–I'll think about it."

Dixie sat back on the bed and drew her legs up under her. "Don't just think. Pray. Why don't we pray about it right now?"

Ashley laughed through her tears. "Girl, what would I do without you?" She swung the pillow at Dixie. "You keep me on the straight and narrow."

"I sure do." Dixie tossed the pillow back at Ashley. "And I'm good for a few laughs, too!"

❧

Ashley felt better after her prayer time with Dixie, but she still couldn't sleep. Too many questions tumbled in her brain; too many conflicting emotions tugged at her heart. *Should I go or stay? Love Tonio or leave him?*

After tossing and turning for an hour, she got up, pulled on her robe, and slipped out to the lanai. The wind was rising off the ocean, rustling the trees, and stirring the grasses with hushed whispers. The lanai groaned and the screened windows creaked as if unseen hands were shaking the cottage.

Ashley gazed out toward the main house. All was quiet and dark. Was Tonio sleeping? Or was he pacing the floor, thinking of her?

Or has he gone to the cliffs again?

A sudden sense of foreboding chilled her. She hugged herself, shivering. The more she thought about it, the more likely it seemed that he would go there tonight. The tabloid show had left him distraught, and perhaps he was regretting the way he had sent her away so harshly. She recalled his words that afternoon on the beach. "*It's as if the devil himself keeps drawing me to the cliff and taunting me to jump into the ocean to make atonement for my sin.*"

"Dear Lord, no," she whispered. "Don't let him do it!"

With growing urgency, she rushed back inside, threw on a shirt, jeans, and sandals, and set out through the woods to the cliffs. As she made her way through palm and mango trees and the thick undergrowth of tropical ferns, the wind whistled through swaying branches and sent little eddies of leaves whirling at her feet. She stepped gingerly among the brambles and twigs, following slivers of moonlight that pierced the dense foliage. Twice she stumbled and caught herself, her breathing labored, her mind playing tricks on her. The forest seemed alive with whispers, its spreading limbs moving, stirring, swaying as if in a hushed requiem of lament. Did all of nature know what she was just beginning to fear—that Tonio's life hung in the balance tonight?

When she finally emerged into the clearing, her first glimpse was of a full moon casting a silver ribbon of light over the rocky cliffs. But her heart caught in her throat as she spotted a dark figure standing at the edge of the precipice.

Tonio!

He stood facing the sea, his arms raised, a liquor bottle in one hand, the wind howling around him.

Ashley moved toward him, slowly, silently, one agonizing step after another. At any moment he could jump and be gone. She resisted the urge to call out to him. If she startled him, he could lose his balance and fall. A twig snapped under her foot. She stopped, holding her breath. But the sound was lost in the eerie whine and moan of the wind.

When she got closer, she spoke his name gently. "Tonio."

He pivoted and stared at her as if waking from a dream. Moonlight and shadows accented his rugged features. His voice was husky with surprise. "Ashley?"

She held out her hands to him. "Please, Tonio, don't do it."

He shook his head, looking bewildered. "Don't do what?"

"Don't listen to the devil's lies. You can't give your life to atone for Brianna's death."

He accepted her outstretched hand. "Is that what you think? That I'm going to jump?"

She searched his shadowed eyes. "Yes. Weren't you?"

The wind whipped his ebony hair and rippled his shirt. "I came here to throw this bottle of booze into the sea. I almost gave in and drank it tonight. All these years I kept it just in case I needed it. I really needed it tonight, but God gave me the strength to resist. Now I'm giving it to Him once and for all." As if to prove his point, he turned and heaved the bottle into the ocean. "There. It's gone. Forever!"

He turned back and opened his arms to her. She eagerly entered his embrace, pressing her head against his strong chest, savoring the delicious warmth of his sturdy arms. "I love you, dearest one," he whispered against her hair.

"Oh, Tonio, I love you, too."

A capricious wind wrapped around them, groaning a disquieting siren song. As they steeled themselves against its gusty blast, Tonio's foot slipped on loose lava rocks lining the craggy shelf. A scream tore from Ashley's throat as the earth beneath their feet gave way. They both scrambled to regain their footing on the cascading gravel. Tonio pushed her hard, propelling her backward, sprawling and dazed, onto the grass.

"Tonio!" Her eyes searched the darkness, her heart jackhammering. *Did he go over? No, no, no!*

"I'm here, Ashley!"

She crawled toward the flinty edge, the taste of salt spray and grit in her mouth. Tonio was there, a shadowed figure grasping a moon-washed boulder, his feet kicking at sheer air. "Get back," he rasped. "It's not stable. It's all going to go!"

"No! Let me help you."

"Go!"

She held out her hand.

As his fingers circled her wrist, the thunder of falling rocks echoed against the roar of the restless ocean below them. His grip was so tight she winced. "Hold on to the rock," he told her, his breathing ragged. With monumental effort, he swung one leg onto the bluff, hoisted himself up onto the rock, and climbed back to solid ground.

They clung to each other for a long moment, trembling. She wept. He kissed her hair. "I think you just saved my life."

"You saved mine first."

He slipped his arm around her shoulders and walked her back to the cottage. Pausing outside her door, he looked down at her and said, "We're both exhausted tonight. But tomorrow we'll talk. We both have a lot to say. For now, good night, love."

❧

At breakfast the next morning, Ashley and Tonio exchanged private glances across the table while Dixie chatted about the souvenirs she wanted to purchase before leaving Hawaii. "I'm going to spend all day in town. You two don't mind, do you? You can come with me, Ashley, if you like. I've mapped out all the stores. I'm getting some more of those chocolate-covered macadamia nuts—they're absolutely delicious!—and I'm dying to get one of those hot pink sarongs to match my bathing suit. And I love those little koa wood bowls. They're great for salads and popcorn. And, of course, I can't leave without some more Kona coffee. What do you think, Ashley? Do you want to come, or would you be totally bored? You've been here so long, you've probably seen everything already, right?"

"I've seen a lot," Ashley agreed. "The truth is, Tonio and I really need to spend the day finishing the edits on his novel."

"Oh, sure, sure you do." Dixie took one last swallow of coffee and stood up. "So I'll get out of your hair and let you guys work, work, work." She paused. "You don't mind if I borrow your car, do you, Tonio?"

"Not at all." He reached in his pocket and handed her the keys. "Have fun. Take all the time you need."

"Thanks, Tonio. I'll bring you guys some sushi or pineapples or coconuts or something."

"Don't worry about us," said Ashley. "Just go!"

Dixie gave a little wave as she headed for the door. "Shop 'til you drop, that's my motto."

When she had gone, Tonio sat back in his chair and laughed. "I know she's your best friend, but I didn't think she'd ever stop talking."

Ashley sipped her coffee. "I know. I felt the same way."

"All I could think about was how much I wanted to be alone with you, free to talk, free to share what's on my heart."

Ashley nodded. "Me, too."

Tonio pushed his plate aside. "I know we have to work on the book, but first we talk, okay?"

She loved the merry glint in his eyes today. "Sounds good to me."

He got up from the table and called into the kitchen, "Thanks for breakfast, Mika. It was great, as usual." He took Ashley's hand and helped her up. "Now let's head for the office for some private time together."

After closing the door behind them, they settled on the sofa facing the wall of windows overlooking the pool area. The sun shone in, suffusing the room with a rosy warmth. Tonio reached over and took her hand. "It's been quite a roller-coaster ride, hasn't it?"

"You mean, our relationship? Or are you talking about the last few days?"

"Both."

He rubbed the back of her hand. "Last night was a wake-up call for me. I was so stupid to go to the cliff like that, as if it were some necessary ritual or rite of passage. When I think that we both could have been killed, I shudder inside."

"I thought you were going to. . ." She let her words drop off.

"Ashley, I would never do that. I'm sorry I put that idea into your head. I realize our relationship has been unconventional, to say the least. You've had to put up with a lot from me. But God has used you in so many ways to reach into my heart and change me. I don't know what I would do without you."

Ashley glanced out toward the pool, where rivers of sunlit diamonds sparkled on its surface. She didn't know what to say to Tonio. She was still struggling for answers. Did God want them together, or did He want her to go back to New York? How could she be sure she was following His will and not just her own wishes?

"You look lost in thought," Tonio noted.

She met his gaze. "I'm sorry. I guess I have a lot on my mind."

He squeezed her hand. "I hope I'm uppermost in your thoughts."

She smiled. "You are. You know you are. But things are so complicated."

"They don't have to be."

"What are you saying?"

He released her hand, sat forward, and massaged his knuckles. "I just want you to know that all the things you've been trying to drum into my thick skull are finally making sense. Last night when I got back to the house I had some time to think. . .and pray. I got out my Bible and read several passages in the Gospel of Mark, especially Mark 12:30, the Great Commandment."

"That's my favorite verse," said Ashley. "It amazes me that God desires our love. He has all of heaven, all of creation, and yet He still wants us to love Him."

"Quite a challenge," said Tonio. "Loving God with all our heart, soul, mind, and strength. I thought a lot about that last night, and I realized what you said about my pride was absolutely correct."

Ashley settled back into the corner of the sofa and tucked her legs under her. "Really?"

"Yeah, really. As long as I kept my eyes focused on myself and my failures, I was putting myself first. And that's selfish. And wrong. That's what I've been doing. And it's kept me from feeling close to God. I couldn't experience His forgiveness when I refused to forgive myself, because in a perverse way I was thinking only of myself, not Him."

"Exactly."

He reached over and rubbed her shoulder. "So now I'm trying to do what you suggested. And what the scripture says. Focus on Jesus. Love Him with everything in me. And everything else is simply in His hands."

"And how does that make you feel?"

He thought a moment. "It makes me feel. . .free. Forgiven. Joyful. As if a huge boulder had rolled off my shoulders into the ocean, never to be seen again. My mind is clear for the first time in years."

"I am so happy for you." He was still massaging her neck. She placed her hand over his, savoring the warmth. She wished they could be together like this forever.

"I owe it all to you, Ashley," he said, his deep voice resonating with emotion. "You didn't give up on me. You helped me get back on track."

"It wasn't me, Tonio. God wooed you back."

"He used you to show me the truth."

She smiled. "I'm grateful I could help."

"There's so much more I want to say, Ashley." He pulled her over beside him, his arm circling her shoulders, his fingertips lightly drumming her arm. Her head rested easily on his chest. She loved being close to him like this, savoring the warmth of his touch, the fresh scent of his aftershave, the nubby texture of his shirt against her cheek. But what would happen to this sweet fellowship when she told him she might go home?

"Ashley, did you hear me?" He pressed his chin against the top of her head.

"What?" With her ear against his chest, she could hear his heartbeat and feel the rumbling, reassuring vibration of his voice.

"I said, we have so much more to talk about. Before, I was so consumed with keeping secrets from you—about Brianna, my drinking, the accident—I couldn't allow myself to think of a future together. But now—now you know everything. And you're still here. Even last night on the cliff you said you loved me, as I love you. You meant it, didn't you?"

"Yes," she murmured, "I do love you."

His arm tightened around her. "And I love you more than I can say." He lifted her face to his and gently kissed her lips. "This is only the beginning, Ashley. It came to me this morning how perfect we are for each other. Maybe it's too soon to speak of marriage—I don't know—but I pray that someday you might consider becoming my wife."

Ashley pulled away from his embrace. She brushed her tousled hair back from her face. "Your wife?"

His brow furrowed. "I spoke too soon, didn't I? Like a fool, I'm rushing headlong into this. Too fast. Too soon. I can see you're upset."

"Not upset. Surprised. A little overwhelmed."

"I'm not asking you today, Ashley. This isn't an official

proposal. It's just something to think and pray about."

"I will. I'll pray about it."

"But you are upset. I can see it in your eyes."

Ashley looked away. "It's just—I don't know what God wants me to do. Since coming to Hawaii, I've let so many things distract me from my relationship with Him."

"You mean me?"

"You. Ben. My work. Everything. It's so easy for everyday life to get in the way. Just like you, Tonio, I'm trying to focus again on my walk with Christ."

"Can't we do that together, Ashley? I can't imagine a better life than that—the two of us serving God together."

She folded her hands under her chin. "It sounds wonderful, but. . ."

"But what?"

"God may have other plans for me."

"What other plans? What are you talking about?"

"I don't know how to tell you this—"

Impatience crept into his voice. "Just say it, Ashley."

"Okay. Here's the thing. I–I've been thinking about going back to New York."

"New York?" Tonio's tone was sharp, incredulous. "You can't be serious."

"It's the truth." She forced out the words. "I'm thinking of flying home with Dixie."

"Is this her idea? Did she talk you into it?"

"No. It's just something I've been thinking about, something I feel the Lord is leading me to do. Our work is done. You've worked through your problems. There's no reason for me to stay."

"There's every reason!" A vein throbbed in Tonio's temple. "I love you, Ashley. You love me."

Hot tears scalded her eyes. "It's not enough, Tonio."

"You're telling me love isn't enough to build a future on? Then what is?"

She brushed away her tears. "I've got to know it's God's will."

Tonio raked his fingers through his hair. "Of course it's His will. Why else do you think He brought us together? He's orchestrated every step of the way."

"I want to believe that, Tonio. I want us to be together. But I don't know if it's God plan or just my own wishful thinking. I made a mistake with Ben. I don't want to make the same mistake again."

He shot her a wounded glance. "I'm not Ben."

"I know."

"Is that the problem? You still want Ben?"

"No, I didn't say that."

"But if God wanted you with Ben, you'd go back to him?"

"I suppose. But this isn't about Ben. It's about us—about what God wants for us."

Tonio stood up and walked over to the window. "All right," he said, an edge in his voice. "Maybe we've both said enough for now. Pray about it, Ashley. I'll pray, too. We'll see what happens. Meanwhile, if you're thinking about going home in a few days, we'd better get back to work on those final edits."

Over the next two days Tonio said nothing about his proposal or their future together. Everything was strictly business. He and Ashley finished the work on his novel and e-mailed the completed manuscript to Ben. Ben replied with a brief e-mail:

> *Congratulations, Tonio! This is a winner. Your best work yet! Good work, Ashley. You've brought out the best in Tonio. You're a great team.*

Reading Ben's e-mail, Ashley couldn't miss the irony in his remarks. If she and Tonio were really such a great team, why was she feeling so conflicted over their relationship? As much as she wanted to stay in Hawaii, and as hard as she prayed that God would give her the peace to stay, she nevertheless found herself packing up her belongings and preparing to go home with Dixie.

Until the very hour that she and Dixie were to leave for the airport, Ashley continued bombarding heaven with prayers that God would show her she belonged with Tonio. But no signs from heaven appeared, no angel of light revealed the road best taken, no vision captured her senses with a certainty that Tonio was the man for her.

In the wake of God's apparent silence, Ashley said good-bye to Anthony Adler and the lovely, romantic, turbulent, mercurial life she had known in Kona. They said good-bye at the airport with a restrained embrace, a minimum of words, and an undercurrent of emotion as tempestuous as a storm-whipped sea.

Ashley's heart broke as Tonio said, "I'll never forget you. You'll always be a part of me."

Fighting back tears, she replied, "You'll always be in my heart, too."

All the way home on the six-hour flight to New York, Ashley's thoughts raged with recriminations and second thoughts. *What on earth are you doing leaving the man you love? What more do you want than a genuine, amazing, fascinating man like Tonio? What more do you expect—a letter of permission from God written in the clouds? What if you've just thrown away your last chance at happiness?*

But as her plane touched down at Kennedy International Airport, Ashley's pulse raced. She was home, in the world she had known for so many years, about to resume the life she had left behind after Ben broke her heart. God was still in charge. He knew her heart. No matter what the future held, she desired to be obedient to Him.

nineteen

Over the next six months, as Ashley settled back into life in New York City, she and Tonio kept in touch by e-mail.

December 23

Tonio, I can hardly believe I've been away from Hawaii for nearly a month. I got my job back at Haricott, working now for another editor. Not Ben—although we pass in the halls and share a cup of coffee in the cafeteria now and then. The snow is falling here in New York, and the streets are strung with festive lights. I'm sitting here in my little apartment with my miniature Christmas tree while icicles hang like crystal stalactites from my windows and two-foot snowdrifts blanket the yard. How I miss Hawaii's sun and surf, the tropical flowers, and all the greenery. Most of all, I miss you.

December 25

Merry Christmas, Ashley. How I wish you were here. I keep looking out at the cottage and expecting to see you there. This big old house feels so empty without you bustling about the office or sitting across from me at dinner or walking with me along the beach. I'm still attending AA, but I'm also getting more involved in my church. I've joined the men's prayer group, and even though I'm a loner at heart, I'm enjoying the fellowship and discovering the power and blessings that come from praying for one another. And, of course, every moment of every day you have my prayers, dear Ashley. . .and my heart.

January 13

Tonio, I can't believe it's a new year already. The snow is still here, deeper than ever. But Hawaii is in my heart. At various times during the day I try to picture what you are doing. Then I remember it's six hours earlier there and you're half a world away. I miss you! By the way, be praying for Ben. We've talked things out. I've vented; he's listened. We've both had to do a reality check on our lives. He seems to be taking his faith seriously. He's often at church these days. Pray that he continues to grow in the Lord.

January 19

Ashley, is there more about Ben you're not telling me? Or don't I have the right to ask?

January 20

Ben and I are in the process of making peace with each other. The wounds are healing. We've agreed to be friends— friends who keep their distance.

February 6

Ashley, it amazes me that I still feel your presence here in this house. Sometimes I walk around my estate and imagine you beside me, enjoying the sunsets, gazing out at the sea, burrowing your toes in the sand. I resist the urge to phone you lest, hearing your voice, I throw caution to the wind and rush to New York to bring you home with me.

February 10

Oh, Tonio, I haven't called you for the same reason. As long as I don't hear your voice, I can pretend you aren't quite real. How I miss you! But God is teaching me to be patient, to wait on Him, to trust that He knows best. My work at Haricott is going well, but it's not as much fun as working for a certain renowned novelist living in Hawaii. I'm *working again on my novel and sending out proposals to Christian publishers. Pray that my novel will find a happy home somewhere.*

March 18

Ashley, I'm so pleased you're back at work on your novel. It's a beautiful story, and I pray it will be embraced by just the right publisher. My novel, Cliffs Over Kona, will be on store shelves next week. For the most part, the reviews are good and presales are strong. I keep thinking about how much you poured yourself into this book. You encouraged me to reach deep within myself and search for truth, no matter how painful. Not only is this a better book because of you—I'm a better person for having known you. I'll forever be indebted to you, my love.

March 29

Tonio, thank you for the autographed copy of your book. It looks beautiful. And I never dreamed that you would dedicate it to me. Thank you! I will treasure it always. . .as I treasure you.

April 4

Ashley, I'll be starting a six-week, multi-city book tour next week. I'll be doing lots of media interviews and book signings. I admit I'm dreading the whole ghastly experience, but 'tis the life I've chosen, so I'd better not complain too loudly. Naturally I'd rather be home writing than living out of dreary hotels and drearier airports. Say a prayer for me. Wherever I may be in the weeks ahead, my heart is still there with you.

May 1

Tonio, I just heard the news. Congratulations on winning the National Golden Pen Award! It looks like our paths will

*be crossing here in New York City when you come to accept
your award. I can't wait to see you again.*

May 3

    *Dear girl, no award will mean half as much to me as
seeing you again. I'm counting the days.*

May 27

    *News item in the New York Times: The National Golden
Pen Awards ceremony will be held at the Waldorf Astoria
at 6:00 p.m., Saturday, May 30th. The literary community
will gather to honor bestselling author Anthony Adler with
first prize for his latest novel,* Cliffs Over Kona. *Adler, who
just completed a national book tour, will give the keynote
address. His novel, which has won rave reviews even among
his harshest critics, is being made into a major motion picture
scheduled for release next year.*

For weeks Ashley had looked forward to this evening. At
times she had awakened in the middle of the night, her heart
pounding at the thought of seeing Tonio again. Now here
she was at the world-famous Waldorf-Astoria Hotel, sitting
beside Ben and Dixie in an opulent ballroom, watching Tonio
receive his award. She hadn't had a chance to talk with him
yet. His plane had been late, so he had come here directly
from the airport, with just enough time to take the stage
for his speech. But they would be together again at the gala
reception after the ceremony. What would she say to him
after all this time?

The ceremony lasted less than two hours, but for Ashley it
seemed eternal. When the final applause died out, she was the
first on her feet. She slipped through the crowd ahead of Ben
and Dixie. Even in her flowing, mint green strapless gown,
with her blond hair styled in a cascade of crimped curls, she
felt tongue-tied and self-conscious as a schoolgirl.

"Wait up, Ash," said Dixie. "We're right here with you, okay?"

"I know. What I don't know is what I'll say or how I'll feel when I see Tonio again. I just might swoon at his feet."

Dixie chuckled. "At least that would make a memorable impression."

"That's not the kind of impression I'm hoping for."

"I know. You want him to take one look at you and wonder why he ever let you out of his sight."

Ashley grimaced. "You know me way too well, Dixie."

"I sure do. You're hoping he'll sweep in and whisk you back to Hawaii on his white steed. Or a jet airplane. Whatever."

"You think?"

"Only you're really afraid when you see him again, nothing will happen, and you'll each keep going your separate ways."

Ashley clasped Dixie's hand. "You guessed it, girlfriend. I walked away from him when I left Hawaii. What if he walks away from me now?"

"It's in God's hands, Ash. He knows what's best for both of you."

"I know. I keep holding on to that thought."

The party was well under way as they entered the festive reception hall. An orchestra was playing and people were mingling and laughing. It promised to be a beautiful night to remember.

"I'm heading for the hors d'oeuvres," said Dixie. "I hope they have some of those little crispy things with cream cheese. Want me to get you guys something?"

"No, I'm fine for now," said Ben.

"Me, too." Ashley scanned the crowd for Tonio. Just as she was about to give up, she turned, and there he was, bigger than life, more handsome than ever in his black tuxedo and tails.

"Tonio!" Her ankles were suddenly weak in her three-inch heels.

"Hello, Ashley." His blue eyes flashed with admiration. "You look stunning as usual."

Her face warmed. "Thank you. So do you."

He embraced her, then handed her a long-stemmed goblet. "I brought you a ginger ale."

She accepted the glass with a little titter of laughter. His closeness left her feeling light-headed and giddy. "You didn't have to do that, Tonio. I should bring you a drink. You're the man of the hour."

"She's right, ol' man," said Ben, extending his hand. "Congratulations on the award. It was well deserved."

"And thank you again for dedicating the book to me," said Ashley. "I never expected that."

"It wouldn't be the book it is today without you, Ashley," said Tonio. "And you, Ben. You two deserve the acclaim as much as I do."

"Now you're being unduly modest," said Ben. "That's not like you, Tonio."

He grinned. "Let's say it's been quite a year of change for all of us."

"Yes, it has," said Ben. "Mostly changes for the good."

Ben turned to Ashley. "Listen, I'm going to go find Dixie and help her carry back those heaping plates of goodies she's no doubt collected."

As Ben walked away, Tonio said, "He's a good man."

Ashley nodded. "Yes, he is."

Tonio's voice deepened. "It's been a long time."

She nodded again. "Six months."

"You never called."

I couldn't bear the pain of hearing your voice again. "Neither did you," she said.

"So many times I almost called you, but, frankly, hearing your voice would have stirred up all the loneliness again." He touched her arm, his eyes looking deep into hers. "I've got to know. Are you happy living in New York? Really happy?"

She looked away, flustered. "Happy? Why wouldn't I be happy?"

He rubbed her arm gently. "I just need to be sure. There's nothing more I want for you than your happiness."

She studied him. "What about you? Are you happy?"

"Sure. I'm content." He cleared his throat. "I've come a long way since last year. God has done a lot of work in my life. I'm not the tormented man I used to be. In fact, I can't complain about anything. God has given me the peace and fellowship with Him I've always longed for."

Ashley's eyes filled. "I'm happy for you, Tonio. That's been my prayer for you every day."

"And I'm happy for you," he said. "It looks like you have the stable life you've always wanted."

She nodded. "I suppose I do. I finished writing my novel."

"Wonderful. The first of many, I hope."

"It's coming out next year with a Christian publishing house in the Midwest. I just found out two days ago. It probably won't be the blockbuster yours is, but I'll be reaching people with the message the Lord has given me."

He squeezed her arm. "I'm so proud of you, Ashley. It sounds like you're living a rather perfect life these days."

"I don't know if I'd call it perfect, but I have a pleasant routine—work, writing, friends, family, church."

He smiled. "What more could you want?"

She sipped her ginger ale. "It's not set in stone, of course. My life, I mean. It could change."

"It could?"

"Yes. I may not always stay in New York."

"Really? You might consider going somewhere else?"

"Of course. I'm always open to a little adventure in my life." *What kind of banal conversation is this?* she wondered. Why couldn't she say what she wanted to say?

Tonio rubbed his jaw. "I'm glad to hear that, Ashley. I am, too. Open, I mean. To a little adventure."

"Your life in Hawaii is quite adventurous, I'd say."

"Yes, I'd say so. Hawaii is a wonderful place for adventure—assuming that's what you're looking for."

"Yes, assuming that, Hawaii is a wonderful place. I loved it there."

"I'm glad you loved it there. I love it, too."

"Quite a coincidence, isn't it?" she murmured.

"A coincidence?"

"Both of us loving Hawaii so much."

A hearty chuckle rose from Tonio's throat. "This is the most confounding conversation I've ever had. Do either of us have the slightest idea what we're talking about?"

The humor in the moment struck Ashley, too. She stifled an urge to grin foolishly. "You're right. We're not expressing ourselves very well. We sound like dunderheads."

"Now there's a word I haven't heard lately. If you mean we're acting like a couple of fools, I heartily agree. Neither of us is admitting what's really on our minds."

He stepped forward and drew her into his arms. He held her close and whispered into her ear, "Here's what I really want to say. Is there still a chance for us?"

She rested her head against his chest. For the first time in over six months she felt at home, in exactly the place she was meant to be. "Yes, Tonio, there's every chance," she replied with a sigh. "I love you more than words can say."

He pressed his lips against her hair. "I never stopped loving you, Ashley. Not for a moment. You were in my heart wherever I went. No matter what I did, you were there."

"I felt the same way," she confessed. "You know I didn't want to leave Hawaii, but I had to. It wasn't God's time for us."

"You were so sure of that."

"No, I wasn't sure at all. It's taken all this time for me to understand why God was holding me back."

"And now you understand?"

"Yes, Tonio. I do. We were two very wounded people back

then. We both needed time to heal. We needed to let God make us whole again without leaning on each other as a crutch."

"If you were a crutch, you were a very lovely one."

She smiled. "You know what I mean. God had special work to do in us. And I think we both let Him do it."

He tipped her face up to his, his eyes twinkling. "Are you saying what I think you're saying, love? Is this God's time for us?"

A smile started in her heart and spread to her lips. "Yes, Tonio, I believe it is."

He cut off her words with a kiss, slow and tender and exquisite. For one glorious moment Ashley forgot they were standing in a banquet hall surrounded by party guests. Then she heard a patter of applause. She looked around, her face heating with embarrassment. Several guests were watching, smiling, clapping.

Amid the applause, Tonio slipped his arm around her waist and held her as if he would never let her go. "I was just thinking, my love," he murmured against her ear, "God willing, September is a wonderful time of year for a wedding in Hawaii."

She looked up at him, thrilling to the love she saw in his eyes. "Yes, sweetheart, God willing, September is a perfect time!"

A Letter To Our Readers

Dear Reader:
In order that we might better contribute to your reading enjoyment, we would appreciate your taking a few minutes to respond to the following questions. We welcome your comments and read each form and letter we receive. When completed, please return to the following:

Fiction Editor
Heartsong Presents
PO Box 719
Uhrichsville, Ohio 44683

1. Did you enjoy reading *By the Beckoning Sea* by Carole Gift Page?
   ❑ Very much! I would like to see more books by this author!
   ❑ Moderately. I would have enjoyed it more if

   _____

   _____

   _____

2. Are you a member of **Heartsong Presents**? ❑ Yes ❑ No
   If no, where did you purchase this book? _____

   _____

3. How would you rate, on a scale from 1 (poor) to 5 (superior), the cover design? _____

4. On a scale from 1 (poor) to 10 (superior), please rate the following elements.

   ____ Heroine   ____ Plot
   ____ Hero   ____ Inspirational theme
   ____ Setting   ____ Secondary characters

5. These characters were special because? _____

_____

_____

6. How has this book inspired your life? _____

_____

_____

7. What settings would you like to see covered in future
   Heartsong Presents books? _____

_____

_____

8. What are some inspirational themes you would like to see
   treated in future books? _____

_____

_____

9. Would you be interested in reading other **Heartsong
   Presents** titles? ❑ Yes ❑ No

10. Please check your age range:

   ❑ Under 18   ❑ 18-24
   ❑ 25-34   ❑ 35-45
   ❑ 46-55   ❑ Over 55

Name _____

Occupation _____

Address _____

City, State, Zip_____

Presents

Great Inspirational Romance at a Great Price!

Heartsong Presents books are inspirational romances in contemporary and historical settings, designed to give you an enjoyable, spirit-lifting reading experience. You can choose wonderfully written titles from some of today's best authors like Wanda E. Brunstetter, Mary Connealy, Susan Page Davis, Cathy Marie Hake, Joyce Livingston, and many others.

When ordering quantities less than twelve, above titles are $2.97 each.
Not all titles may be available at time of order.

SEND TO: **Heartsong Presents** Readers' Service
P.O. Box 721, Uhrichsville, Ohio 44683

Please send me the items checked above. I am enclosing $ _____
(please add $4.00 to cover postage per order. OH add 7% tax. WA add 8.5%). Send check or money order, no cash or C.O.D.s, please.
To place a credit card order, call 1-740-922-7280.

NAME _____

ADDRESS _____

CITY/STATE _____ ZIP_____

HP 11-08